circa

BOOKS BY DEVI S. LASKAR

FICTION
circa
The Atlas of Reds and Blues

POETRY
Anastasia Maps
Gas & Food, No Lodging

ANTHOLOGIES
Taboos & Transgressions: Stories of Wrongdoings
(co-edited with Luanne Smith
and Kerry Neville)

Graffiti
(co-edited with Pallavi Dhawan
and Tamika Thompson)

circa

DEVI S. LASKAR

MARINER BOOKS
Boston   New York

Lucille Clifton, excerpt from "i am accused of tending to the past" from *The Collected Poems of Lucille Clifton*. Copyright © 1991 by Lucille Clifton. Reprinted with the permission of The Permissions Company, LLC, on behalf of BOA Editions, Ltd., boaeditions.org.

CIRCA. Copyright © 2022 by Devi S. Laskar. All rights reserved. Printed in the United States of America. No part of this book may be used or reproduced in any manner whatsoever without written permission except in the case of brief quotations embodied in critical articles and reviews. For information, address HarperCollins Publishers, 195 Broadway, New York, NY 10007.

HarperCollins books may be purchased for educational, business, or sales promotional use. For information, please email the Special Markets Department at SPsales@harpercollins.com.

FIRST EDITION

Designed by Suet Y. Chong

Library of Congress Cataloging-in-Publication Data has been applied for.

ISBN 978-0-358-65292-2

22 23 24 25 26 LSC 10 9 8 7 6 5 4 3 2 1

For

Susan M. Freiburg

1960–1996

Shine on, Sissy

this past was waiting for me
when i came

—Lucille Clifton,
"i am accused of tending to the past"

circa

Blue jean dreams

YOU LIVE IN YOUR STAR-SPANGLED DESIRES LIKE A DREAM. You want to wear blue jeans the color of the moonlit sky at midnight. To pirouette in red suede shoes, warm in a white sweater you once saw on a mannequin at the expensive mall, your wavy hair out of its fish-scale braids, down past your waist again, kept in place by a silver tinted barrette the shape of a butterfly. You want to appear to be a quintessential American girl. Just like Katrina, the only freshman voted on the homecoming court two years ago—except with a perfect, sun-kissed complexion. In your daydream, your parents' refrain is never "No, Heera. No!" when you ask for a high school yearbook or a transistor radio. In your dream, you and your parents do not shout at each other over whether the printed batik salwar kameez the colors of parrot feathers is suitable school attire. You do not fling across the room the handmade leather sandals that are better matched for the arid climate of Kolkata, not high school in the verdant suburbs of Raleigh, galleries of pine trees at every turn. In the dream, you wear mascara, talk for hours on a telephone in your room to your best friend Marie, and kiss Marie's older brother Marco on Saturday nights when he picks you up for a date in his father's vintage Chevy. In the dream, you are American: not Heera Sanyal with a multitude of prefixes and hyphens and expectations in the shape and weight of a shifting subcontinent thousands of miles away.

Sleight of hand

M A SEPARATES THE DRAPES AND ALLOWS THE STICKY SUN-shine to pour into your bedroom. Its concentrated white light shoots across your face.

"Did you forget something?" Ma asks, her Bengali softly spoken, tranquil. She slings the pearl-embroidered, magenta salwar kameez on top of your crumpled sheets, the long tunic and matching pants still encased in plastic from the dry cleaner's. You picture the pasty-faced proprietor who always asks where you're from and you always answer, "Born in New York and raised in Raleigh."

You'd agreed to pick up your clothes yesterday but had forgotten. Clothes she procures from India, brings back in suitcases from friends returning to the United States; clothes she procures from New York's Little India—that her friends deposit in plastic shopping bags on your scarred wooden coffee table in the living room. You hold up your hand like a visor yet you can't see the details of her face, just the outline of her form next to the sun. "I'm sorry," you mumble in English.

"You'll need this for tonight's party at the Chatterjees' house," she says, ordering you to switch to Bengali.

You reside in America but it is the India of your ma and baba's past where you live day to day. You blink until everything comes back into focus: a good day for your mother, her hair washed and smelling of hibiscus oil; she is sporting crimson lipstick and a simple cotton sari with razor-sharp pleats. It is the weekend so she is out of her work clothes — synthetic saris with matching cardigans that make her look like a seasoned stewardess on Air India and not a reference librarian in Wake County.

You don't want to go out with them tonight; you are tired of performing the perfect smile, the graceful manners, the light laughter as the adults at the party repeat the same questions and offer you sugar-free candy, these people whom you have always called uncle and auntie, these people who are suspicious of everything non-Indian in origin, these people who coach your parents how to raise you.

"I've got too much work for school. I can't spare the time." You rise, throw off the hand-stitched quilt, and stumble over your bedroom slippers that are two sizes too small, pink and plush and so precious you cannot part with them.

"Well, you can't replace our friends. These people are our family," Ma says, her body looming behind you on the staircase, her toes brushing your heels. "Our only relatives in America."

You know their stories, Ma and Baba are not shy about sharing their stories with you, about retelling their histories, about retelling you what to think, to forget your own struggles, to concentrate on the lessons that can be learned from theirs. In the evenings, their hands warming over cups of milky cha, they hiss their stories at you, about world war and sacrifice and going without as they deny you permission to babysit to earn money for that yearbook that has become so important to you. On the weekends after a truncated call to India, they hiss their stories at you about their ancestors, the ones who died over a slight and remain unavenged, the ones who lost their husbands, the ones who lost their homes — their struggles led to your survival, their struggles led to victory, living in America. But they are afraid that you'll become too American, that you'll forget everything they ever tried to teach you, that you'll abandon your shared language and culture, that you'll forget the things they hold in the highest esteem. They do not want you to try out for swim & dive; they do not want you to be a part of any American team.

"Money is better spent in India," Ma says. "So many aunties with health problems." She opens the lid to the porcelain sugar bowl and extracts a couple of cubes, drops them into her mug.

"So much money required for medicines and doctor visits for the uncles as well," Baba adds, offering her his thin stirring spoon. The bowl and spoon part of an anniversary gift set sent by cousins to celebrate your parents' two decades of marriage. So many expenses, and their American dollars stretch further than any rupee ever could, so many promises that need to be kept. He works in finance, for a textile factory in the next town. These are the stories repeated to you and to those few who are like you, children of Indian immigrants, born in America but raised to live with one eye toward the day your parents left India—the past flattening to a photograph, one forever frozen in time.

You make a show of the stacks of textbooks you need to complete all of your homework, piling them onto the dining room table. A thin layer of dust on the otherwise pristine wood and you glance at the living room, everything in its place yet static. You can see the particles floating in the air where the amber light shines through the window. It is straightened up but not clean, so uncharacteristic for your parents to leave their home in this condition. Ma frowns. Baba changes out of his dhuti and comes downstairs. "Stay home," he says, his Bengali gentle. They go to the Chatterjees' party without you, and while they're gone you finish your history homework in record time, conjugate all the Spanish verbs on the list, finish the rough draft of the chemistry lab report, then invite Marie and Marco over.

When you were younger, you and Marie took swim lessons together, ate lunch afterward at the picnic benches across the street from the aquatic center, hung upside down from the jungle gym bars for what seemed like hours until you saw nothing but the Milky Way hovering before your eyes. But after the Grimaldis' reaffirmation ceremony (wedding reenactment, as Ma called it), the swim days changed to lessons only, no lunch. You and the Grimaldi kids continue to go to school together, but you can't go camping with them on the weekends, and even at their birthday slumber parties, you are the only one whose parents come to fetch you after the cheese pizza and grilled hot dogs.

"We don't know what people are like at night," Ma had said. "Who knows what could happen?" Ma imagines that out of her sight there are men everywhere, waiting to ruin you and shame the family name.

Tonight, Marco and Marie bring chocolate chip cookies their mother baked and Marco adds a bit of the vodka he stole out of his father's liquor cabinet to the orange juice in your coffee cup. You take a sip and quickly put it down, unable to hide your grimace. The cookies, however, are thin and crispy and taste like the gold in sunshine. Your mother makes samosas with cauliflower-cashew filling from scratch on Sunday afternoons because they are Baba's favorite, but turns up her nose at chocolate and American desserts.

The three of you watch a film about a boy whose dog becomes rabid and he has to shoot him. Marie flinches when the gun is fired, while Marco finishes your drink. You shoo them out after the movie is over, and fluff the couch cushions, take out the trash, wipe down the kitchen counter.

You feign sleep when Baba's car pulls into the driveway, the headlights crossing the walls of your room like shooting stars.

↳↲

Ma and Baba acknowledge your love of the ocean, and admit their awe of it, too. The next weekend, instead of dinner at the Dasguptas' down in Fayetteville, they drive you hours to Nag's Head, a cooler in the trunk. A cheap motel seaside, two creaky double beds and a picture window with an unobstructed view of the shore. Ma makes chicken biriyani on a glorified hotplate in the bathroom. Baba helps you scoop out sand to dig a moat for the small castle you build on the last morning. Ma tells you about the trip she took with her parents when she was the age you are now, to the seaside town of Puri, and the kathi rolls she bought from the street vendor at India's Golden Beach.

"My mind is always there," Ma says as she leans back on the motel lounge chair covered by a faded-starfish-print beach towel from home.

Baba smiles in agreement. "All else is illusion."

On the way back, homework piled on your lap, you close your eyes and think of Marco, how he held your hand on the sofa, traced circles with his thumb on your skin.

"I've never known anyone to waste so much time as you."

You open your eyes to catch Baba shaking his head. "I'm just resting."

"You've spent the whole weekend resting," he says. "You only swam in the ocean for a few minutes."

The car ride turns stuffy. "I'm thinking about my homework, all the papers I have to turn in before next week." A lie. Another lie, your mouth is full of them like teeth.

One hand on the steering wheel, Baba reaches down behind Ma's seat, pulls out a paper bag. "Open it."

A couple of cereal bars and a tepid bottle of orange-flavored sports drink. Unexpected treats. "Thanks, Baba."

He nods. "When you're done, you'll have to give me twenty-five capitals."

"All right," you say, in between bites. Baba is the intellectual equivalent of an army sergeant demanding push-ups. Ever since sixth grade, you've been doing Baba's pop quizzes in world geography. He claims he can still remember every state and national capital he learned in an Indian classroom thirty-five years before. You are required to keep up. Especially now that you're not too far from the high school finish line.

"Ghana?" his voice intones.

"Accra." You think of Mr. Grimaldi, his baseball cap thrown on backwards, playing catch with Marco in their backyard on the weekends, punching his mitt to break it in. You consider how Marco has his dad's easy smile.

Baba grunts. "Morocco?"

You sigh. Too easy. Your stomach growls again, so loud Ma glances back at you for a moment. "Rabat."

Baba briefly grins at you through the rearview mirror. "Maldives?"

He was on an African–Middle East bent for a while, but now he switches regions. Asia. "Male."

He switches lanes. "Good, good. You've been practicing."

Maps

YOUR STORY DOES NOT BEGIN WITH YOU; IT INEVITABLY BE-gins with your parents. And their story does not begin with them. Rather, your story begins with a friendship almost a century ago, on a different continent, long before you were a possibility. Your story begins with your grandfathers' and great-uncles' friends, the ones who walked to school together from their village on the outskirts of what is now West Bengal. Your story begins as these boys grew up and moved out of the village and into the cities to pursue their education, and eventually lost track of one another with the advent of Independence and Partition and famine and migration. Your story begins with a chance encounter between your maternal and paternal grandfathers, old friends of said village or villages who had not seen each other in thirty years. Your story begins when they recognize each other on a crowded Kolkata street, and the fateful words are uttered: *I have a son,* and *I have a daughter.* That's that.

Your story, though, really begins when your parents marry and your father applies for that fellowship right after the wedding. Your parents leave their continent, their subcontinent, their country, their province, their village, their enclave, their families, their friends, everything they ever knew or recognized or loved, behind.

*

Some twenty years before as the position of the stars overhead changed, Ma and Baba lost their place along the dirt roads and pathways carved by the rubber wheels of the buses and sandaled feet of the millions in their home city. They no longer stood in the congested alleys or hung on to crowded buses or waded through the marketplace, no longer breathed the air thick with mosquitoes and flies and bees, incense from the public temples mingling with the kiosks where street food was cooked over open flames and sold for almost nothing. They no longer heard the continuous sounds of bickering and laughing from every open window, songs playing on competing radios, a government sanctioned voice over a loud-speaker in the distance extolling the virtues of socialism.

You know their loneliness as they boarded their first airplane and flew west, first to the bright, empty, and indifferent airport of Frankfurt, then to the international airport in New York. It is the hiss of a bicycle tire going flat as they describe their first moments in America. Far fewer people, all who wore tight clothes, and the women talked as much as the men, their language traveling faster than the airplane they'd stepped out from. You hear again the story of your parents seeing a Black man in person for the first time, as he stood in line ahead of them and ordered a cup of Joe, how they didn't know what that meant. You know how they ordered the same, and were presented with bitter coffee, opaque and sugarless; how they couldn't drink the hot brew, and mourned the loss of their converted currency, their mouths parched, their desires unquenched as the vendors shook their heads and said there was no tea.

You know nothing remained the same for them, your ma and baba, from the minute they'd left India, their parents reluctant to give their blessings, extracting promises that they return promptly, that they return before the children came along and anchored them to a different continent and a different life.

Yet you arrived, and everyone's dreams shifted. You arrived, in New York, on Halloween 1969. Woodstock had happened and so had Neil Armstrong's walk on the moon. But you don't know any of that until later.

You return to India with them, infrequently, brief summer stays that leave your parents wistful, unsatisfied, making more promises to return, and then doing the mathematics of moving back and begging off. It has been years since you last visited and there are plans in the works to go before you leave for college.

゛゛

And yet, your own loneliness is foreign to them. They shout as they leave the discount Shoe Barn without paying for the athletic shoes you need for PE. "These are not necessities," Ma says, her voice now carrying several car lengths in the parking lot. The sun wanes in the sky and you cannot see anything but the flash of heat in her eyes, her cheeks pinched from fatigue. She works overtime these days, she comes home in the evenings too tired to cook, and the three of you eat discount sugar-cereal in grimacing silence. From the periphery, you see Marie and her mother entering the shoe store. Mrs. Sanyal and Mrs. Grimaldi do not like each other, yet Ma loves Marie and Mrs. Grimaldi thanks you when she sees you, for being such a good friend to both her son and daughter. You see Marie leave her mother by the boots aisle and appear by your parked car, wordlessly.

"I'm tired of seeing the vice principal at lunch," you snap at your mother, not wanting another lecture on inappropriate clothes and shoes, not wanting that old man's eyes running sprints over your shifting form, your breasts that have bloomed early.

"My mother said the best runners touch the soles of their feet to the earth," Ma says. Her back straight, she is suddenly tall. Like Baba, Ma is an orphan. The people who promised your parents in marriage to each other are all ash and photographs. Although Baba and Ma hail from bigger families, so many uncles and aunts and cousins, they are each like you—an only child.

Your eyes betray you. "Your mother lived eight thousand miles away and never had to smell Mr. Richard's pastrami Reuben on rye twice a week." You do not wipe away your stray tears.

Marie squeezes your hand but nods in understanding at your mother.

Mrs. Sanyal tightens the belt around her peacoat. "Baba and I purchase you the finest things money can buy, Heera."

"In India," you say. "Those things don't work here."

Your father unlocks the door to the car, glares at you and then at his wife. "I did not leave everything behind to adopt the easy-come-easy-go attitude prevalent in America."

He begins his standard lecture on education as a lifeline, as the only ladder out of your family's tight financial circumstances. He does not concede on the shoes, he merely muses aloud that athletic shoes are not the issue, it's your poor attitude. "Ultimately it will reflect badly if she cannot even enter Princeton or Harvard because she cannot persuade the principal—"

You start to argue. "I have no interest in—"

Your mother says goodbye to Marie and commands you to get in the car. "Perhaps boarding school is the answer." Ma's voice is low now, almost a murmur. "There's a good one in Jaipur. She could stay with my cousin."

You slip your hand into your pocket, finger the crisp twenty-dollar bill you lifted from your mother's purse while she made breakfast this morning, and roll it into the shape of a cigarette. Marco taught you how to roll up a bill without looking. You picture the school day, the way the Norton sisters, April Stewart, and even Katrina for that matter, repeat themselves: the smirks at your embroidered kurti tops, eye rolls at homemade chapati egg wraps that your mother insists you eat for lunch, the perpetual questions about the red bindi women like your mother wear ("Is that blood?") and whether cows that roam unimpeded are worshipped ("So you have mobile churches, then?"). You think of the way the Kaminski brothers elongate your name, "Heeeeee-raah," every morning as you cross the visitors' lobby and then rhyme it with *Hee Haw*, a country music variety show on television that your parents love to watch Sunday evenings.

The bill no longer feels heavy. You slide the money to the palm of your hand. Because your mother hates it when you hug any American, you shake hands with Marie, and watch your friend walk back to the store, alone, the bill stuck to her skin.

"I just want them to stop teasing me," you say from the backseat.

"Stop being so sensitive," Baba says. He exits the parking lot onto the narrow two-lane road but without turning on the headlights. A passing car honks. "When they tease you, it means they like you."

The next day Marie comes in to PE with a pair of cheap sneakers dangling by the shoelaces in one hand and Marco's navy sweatpants from seventh grade in the other. You are so grateful.

"Christmas has come early," she says, handing you the loot and then fishing in her pocket for the change.

Cereus cactus

YOU BLOOM AT NIGHT.

Marco calls but Ma says into the receiver you are busy for the next couple of years until you go to college, that perhaps he should finish his senior year by studying. You are awake as Baba falls asleep in front of the TV, the public television channel host droning on and on about some shift in Reagan's foreign policy ahead of his vice president seeking to replace him next year. You check and learn Ma is already asleep, snoring into her pillow, her small black and white broken. She has not been able to convince Baba to have it repaired. He insists he can fix it himself, and yet all of his efforts to date have resulted in a grease stain on the carpet and a roll of aluminum foil wasted. You clean your room, stridently, making sure you stand atop your chair to drop your history textbook onto the ground—for the loud thud. Baba is startled awake and grudgingly rises, turns off the TV in the den with dark wooden paneling and orange shag carpet, and staggers to the master bedroom. You wait until he turns on the shower, then you turn off your bedroom light and slip downstairs to the laundry room. You put a load of wet towels into the dryer then close the back door behind you, shoes in hand. There is an envelope with your name on it in the mailbox: you open it and find a blank yellow piece of paper stuffed inside. It is a sign that Marco will be out tonight.

He pulls up alongside you in his old Honda as you are set to walk across a big intersection, and then follow the access road toward the bus depot.

"Water tower or Merrick's?" he asks, after you exchange smiles and strap on the seat belt. There are still a few untouched water towers in Raleigh, ones you have not yet decorated with anarchy symbols in stolen red paint. It is a clear night, and there are a few friends of Marco's meeting up for beers and smokes behind Mr. Merrick's convenience store and gas shop. You do not care for these boys or the cigarettes, but they leave you alone since you are Marco's friend.

Marco is the kind of boy who worships precision, the kind who, when asked to draw the night sky, enters Mr. Grimaldi's unused library and looks in a worn atlas to put every star in every constellation in its proper place. He could recite Puck's monologue from *A Midsummer Night's Dream* by the time he turned eleven. His appetite for the encyclopedia's contents was so great, he mouthed the words when his voice grew hoarse from the recitations to the walls and the chairs and the empty rooms. He is that kind of boy, wasted on his parents, wasted on the neighborhood boys and their adventures riding through the woods on their bikes, and their makeshift kingdoms in the tree houses just beyond the reach of civilization. He is the child magician who is able to distract everyone and somehow convince them he really could swallow a bird and spit out a mouthful of coins.

It is *Lord of the Flies* but without the fat boy and the slow starvation; to you, he is a picture of wanton freedom. There is a hierarchy among those boys, as there are fiefdoms in every elementary school class, and in every school cafeteria and playground, every junior high and high school, but it wasn't anything physical. All

of the boys look roughly the same. It is Marco's mind that everyone admires and envies, the way he turns a phrase, his exuberant
laughter.

You turn your head and look into the backseat, empty.
"Where's Marie?"

Marco shrugs. "Mom has her doing some chores at home."

The tension in his voice is taut, so you lower your voice and
ask kindly, "Punishment for what?"

He shrugs again. "I siphoned some gas. She took the bullet
for me."

You stare. "They believed her?"

Marco grunts. "She has a way of convincing anyone of anything."

You map yourself, and Marco and Marie, across Raleigh.
There are the water towers that stretch like alien life forms off
Highway 54, from Apex to Cary to Morrisville, where the first
Hindu temple is under construction. Your parents' friends are
thrilled, but you believe what you overhear when you eavesdrop
on white people, at the grocery, by the gas pumps, outside the
library: that this monument to peace and religious tolerance is not
welcome, that the opening of this temple will invite those hooded
boys who proudly wave their Confederate flags and buy billboards
proclaiming North Carolina as *Klan Country* to march in and burn
everything to the ground.

You consider the mall that opened last year, and there is
something wholly American about wasting hours in this place.
You and Marie and Marco sometimes go to ride up and down
the escalators and look at the impeccably attired mannequins in
the storefront windows, grab orange soda from the food court and
split doughy pretzels, warm out of the oven that rotates like a spit,

covered with salt crystals as big as the diamonds that dot their mother's wedding band.

Once, not too long ago, you and Marie walked arm in arm, gasping in mock horror at the price of designer heels, black and spiky. "Are you sure they're shoes?" Marco had asked. "You can turn them upside down and they'd make handy weapons."

You smiled at Marco but when Marie turned to look at you, you were as somber as a nun in church, quick to hide your split allegiance.

"You have no sense of fashion," Marie said to Marco, gravely.

Then both of them looked back at you. You calculated in your head how many kameez sets, how many pairs of sandals you could buy in Kolkata for the single pair of heels that Marie inspected. You could not help it, the calculations, your parents' blood courses inside you. But you had sense enough to omit these figures to the outside world, even Marie. You shrugged in response, palms up, but laughed as they jostled each other. The moment shattered when mall security stopped you at the exit, and demanded that you —just you—empty your pockets, that someone had complained that you've been shoplifting. You were silent when Marco began to argue with the security guard—frozen as you thought back: had you unconsciously helped yourself to something?

Marie was the one who instantly agreed to the guard's demand, and you blushed even as your pockets came up empty. "Now will you apologize?" Marie asked the man, her voice unhurried.

The balding man's scalp went pink and he offered a somewhat sincere apology, to Marie you insisted later, because he wouldn't even look at you.

Marco kicked an empty soda can he found on the ground next to the outdoor trash bin all the way back to the car, sullen.

Once you were safely seated, Marie leaned forward from the

backseat. "Abracadabra," she said. She produced the heels, one from each of her deep coat pockets.

Marco yelled, "Yes!" and the three of you laughed and cheered.

He asks you now, again, adding, "Or how about the mall?"

The mall is not far, you often walk to it on your own, but you do not go inside without both of them. You frown. "Let's try the bus station tonight."

"There's nobody at the local stop," Marco says, waving your suggestion away as if it were a bee.

"Not that one," you say. "The Greyhound station. Better prospects." You tell him to take Hillsborough Street down to Wade Avenue, the lights should all be green at this time of night. You relay you've been studying photographs of the bus station and other public transport centers as part of the *Get to Know Your State* exhibit at the public library: lighting, crowd size, and the rows of navy blue bucket seats with oval cutouts on the backs. Perfect for lifting wallets from the back pockets of travelers. You have been practicing picking pockets on your parents since last spring, after Ma and Baba refused to let you try out for the swim team. But your father's wallet and your mother's purse have become unprofitable, mostly bills with Washington's and Lincoln's faces on them.

Marco smiles. "That's my girl."

Costume jewelry

I T IS THE MORNING OF THE HALLOWEEN CARNIVAL AND MARIE
has stolen an old pirate's costume from her brother's closet to
keep you, her best friend, from running away.

Again.

This attempt again with Marco, the book-smart shaman, the
impractical guide.

Marie does not want to go and she does not want the two of
you to leave. She does not want to be left behind.

"I'll negotiate a small reprieve," Marie tells you and Marco
when he catches up with you both a block and a half from your
house. Marco peeks inside the canvas bag and complains there is
little honor left among thieves. "Maybe your mother will take pity
and let you out tonight."

Your parents had found yet another wallet, worn leather
with no cash, and pictures of gap-toothed children and reminder
cards for dentist appointments—stashed behind the donation box
in your bedroom closet. There had been cash inside that wallet,
money going toward the great escape to New York, but luckily
you had already given the Jacksons and Lincolns to Marco before
taking home the wallet for further study. This time your parents
were like night-blooming cacti, and threatened to call their ex-
tended families in Kolkata. This time they threatened to send you

to India for the coming winter break. One way. This time they threatened to set aside their disdain for publicity to accuse the Grimaldi parents of bad parenting, of allowing their son to act as an accomplice.

"The rules are different for Americans, Heera," Baba had said, wagging his finger in your face.

"I'm American," you insisted.

Both parents shook their heads in unison.

"Only by birth," he said.

You scoffed.

"You have everything," Ma had said. "Why do you act like a thief?"

"You're the only one of us who has true courage, Mario," you say as you step out onto the sidewalk bleached ghost white by the late October sun. "You're the only one willing to take the blame."

You and Marco know Marie participates in the pickpocketing, the water tower graffiti, the funds collection for the great escape. But mostly she is your alibi and foil. Her sweet nature fools everyone.

"Don't move," Marie says to her brother, his face haggard. "Cashing your savings bond and jumping on a train to New York is not the smartest plan." She picks off imaginary lint from his windbreaker.

"Your mother doesn't scare me," she adds, jabbing you in the ribs, trying to frighten away the cloud of disappointment that is already settling around you like a shroud. "Well, not too much."

You smile and Ma pops into your head, when she was driving you home in the rain last fall: how she cursed at the traffic light, thumped the brakes and missed hitting the expensive English car by inches, how she apologized minutes later, how your heart raced faster as she repeated "sorry, sorry" than when the car nearly collided with another's.

"Marie, you're lucky you get to go tomorrow," Marco says, the breeze cold despite the sun. Your birthday dinner is the following evening: Indian families and old connections from all over North Carolina and as far away as Florida are coming for the weekend, sleeping on couches and in sleeping bags, gobbling up the famous shrimp malai curry and tandoori chicken Ma makes every year. Marie is the only school friend invited. "Maybe we shouldn't push it."

The real fun of the weekend, a Halloween festival with school friends, is set for later today.

Your mother has already said no.

"Their answer will remain a no if we don't try one last time," Marie says. "Besides, I thought you two were hitting the train station tonight? Heading to New York?"

"Just a thought," you say.

"Mr. Sanyal hates me." Marco pronounces your last name, your father's last name, perfectly as he eyes the empty road, a string of silver cars parked inches from the painted green curb.

"You ruined his favorite book," Marie replies, turning her back to her brother and allowing you to lead the way home. You notice the frozen flames of Chinese maple, and oaks that tower above the steeples in the corner churches in the Chestnut Hills subdivision. The distance is not far from the Grimaldis' to your house. If it were TV land, you'd be next-door neighbors: their *Brady Bunch* house viewed just before yours, Samantha's house in *Bewitched*.

Marco scowls. "I was ten years old."

Your shared memory of a younger version of Marco coveting illustrations, maps of Antietam from the dusty historical tome Baba had bought at a yard sale years before. Marco had ripped out the illustrations and taken them home, leaving jagged edges in place. The book was returned. Although Marco's family offered apologies and reimbursement ("he's just a child" was the tired refrain), Baba has been holding a grudge.

"He was a prodigy," you say, then grin.

It began as dare between you and Marco, who could lift the most money from their respective parents without being caught. To pay for the ice creams and candy neither family wanted you to have. To pay for cassettes of music neither family wanted you to listen to. Quickly it escalated to who was better at sneaking out of the house at night, who could deface street signs with more artistry, how many trinkets could be had from the dollar store and the pharmacy. It was never enough with Marco, and you loved that about him.

You practiced the art of pickpocketing with clothes on a hanger hooked to the bar above the tub, steaming from the heat of the shower. Marco gleaned strategy from his chess books.

"It's like you're related or something," Marie says.

You laugh.

Everyone knew your parents no longer liked Mr. and Mrs. Grimaldi, had not approved of their marriage or their parenting styles. They had made no secret of it, especially with you. "He's . . . divorced," Ma said in between sips of her cha one Saturday morning. "And she never tells them no." The second Mrs. Grimaldi was much younger and doted on her "Italian twins," as she called her son and daughter, who were hardly a year apart. "She lets the children go wild, even at the library."

You know something else, something about a photograph at a Fourth of July party, years ago, before Ma and Mr. Grimaldi were both graduate students—your mother standing close to a pretty brunette and Marco's father, a rare cat-eating-canary grin on her face. A photograph the size of an index card tucked in between the pages of your mother's favorite prayer book, something she reaches for almost every day.

But it was Baba who explained the importance of that photo to you one day soon after you discovered it. You relaxed on the couch waiting for Ma to return from the bank so you could all go out for pizza. Baba was hunting for something near Ma's prayer book. "I know you found this," he said to you. "You didn't put it back in the right place." He smiled, handing you the photo, and sat beside you.

"They were good friends, Mr. Grimaldi and his first wife and your mother," Baba said. "In New York. Our neighbors." Baba said Sophia didn't want children and didn't want to leave her family in New York. "Ma tried to persuade them to stay together." Baba paused, cleared his throat. "But it didn't work out."

You stared at the woman who could have been your best friends' mother. "Do Marco and Marie know?"

Baba shrugged. "It's not our place to tell them, sona."

This made sense. You touch the pretty lady in a blue sundress, sunglasses perched atop her head. "What does she do now?"

Baba hesitated. "I'm not certain when—"

Ma walked in at that moment and stopped by the foot of the stairs. "Help!" she cried out, two bags wobbling in her arms.

Baba leapt to his feet and moved quickly toward her. "Did you rob the bank?" he asked as he took what appeared to be the laden paper bag.

Ma laughed. "No, I stopped at the Italian grocery. I thought we could make pizza at home."

You stood and offered her the photo. "I'm sorry I looked at your photo."

The smile faded from Ma's lips but she remained gracious. "I keep it to remember her."

After the incident with Baba's history book almost eight years ago, Mr. and Mrs. Grimaldi had thrown a party to celebrate their anniversary and reaffirm their vows, and then head off for a lavish trip to Italy and Greece. They had invited you and your parents to the party—it was the last time both families had come together, at the botanical gardens by the university in Durham. You remember the ride over, how Baba broke the silence by complaining of the endless, perpetual construction on I-40, how Ma murmured in agreement before telling him to take Davis Drive to avoid some college game traffic. You remember staring out the window, prickly in your stiff pink long dress, the canopy of old pines rushing by as the car traversed the narrow road.

Ma's congratulations were scripted in public, warm and gently spoken. Baba shook Mr. Grimaldi's hand and clapped him on the back. The Grimaldis were picture perfect in their stylish attire, tuxedos for the boys and long dresses made from white lace for the girls.

When you got home, your belly full of lasagna and angel food cake with raspberry sauce, Ma told you that your family upheld traditional Indian values, especially loyalty, and she did not want her only child influenced by a divorcé or a permissive American woman who wasted money. Even if they did have a golden-haired daughter with exemplary manners.

You lead Marie to the house, and through the back door. You hold your breath as Marie's cloudless sky blue eyes pierce through the disapproval that hangs over your mother like a halo.

"She wants to wear some *I Dream of Jeannie* outfit that is inappropriate," Ma says.

You kick the back of the chair with your shoe. "I said I wouldn't wear the harem pants . . ."

Marie takes out her brother's things from a plastic grocery bag. "Look, ma'am," she says, pointing to the long sleeves of the pirate blouse, the oversized vest, the ugly riding pants the color of the back end of a lion. "They cover everything."

Your mother sighs. "Ma-rie," she says, stretching the two syllables as far apart as her lips would take her. "Life is not a party." She smoothes the back of her braided bun, and swats away an imagined moth. "You will have some tea," she says as usual to anyone and everyone who walks through the door.

Marie says please and thank you and sits down, even though she hates tea. She takes the cream cracker your mother offers but doesn't bring it to her lips.

Your mother pours the tea but doesn't offer any to you. "Your mother will be there?"

"No, ma'am," Marie says, taking a noisy sip. "My parents are busy."

You feel your mother's eyes boring into your heart. You force yourself to remain still, force yourself to look at the blank wall and mimic its indifference.

Your mother purses her lips as if she had just tasted lemon. "How will you get home?"

"I will call my family," Marie says, careful not to mention her parents, her brother. "Cross my heart, hope to die, she will be safe."

You watch your mother staring at Marie's beauty, a mane of gold-colored hair cascading over her shoulders.

"Ma-rie, you are a good girl, for asking, for knowing your place," Ma says, then picks up her cup of tea, steam rising from the dark liquid. "Perhaps you could speak to my daughter and teach her to accept hers."

Tornado eye

YOU CLICK THE HEELS OF MARIE'S FAUX RUBY SLIPPERS AND wish the afternoon would never end.

The borrowed dress scratches your skin, but you enjoy licking your fingers and rubbing away faint argent lines crisscrossing your arms. Glitter reddens the bathroom floor. After Marie buttons up the blue-and-white-checkered gingham in the back, you want to rake your hands to the unreachable spot between the shoulder blades to quell the sudden itch.

You settle for stuffing more straw into Marie's jute tunic and tightening her braided belt made from fake twine. "I can't wear this for very long," you say, watching the sun begin its slow descent through the opaque glass. You are glad you remembered to bring extra clothes—just in case—stashed in your bag, something to change into at the end of the evening before Mrs. Grimaldi drives you home to Ma and Baba, who are expecting to see you in a pirate's costume.

"Please," Marie says. "I really want a picture of us."

Katrina, Marie's family friend, looks away from her own reflection in the theater barn girls' bathroom, and smirks. She calms the unruly wisps of hair peeking out from her red bandana, places the pirate's patch carefully over her left eye, and touches the smooth blade of the cardboard sword, covered in tinfoil. "Stop complaining, Diamond," Katrina says, brandishing her sword at the two of you across the narrow space of the girls' bathroom.

"I'm not," you begin to say. Your given Bengali name means Diamond. Everyone in your school knows what it means and knows you hate it. What everyone does not know is that your grandmother chose your name. Katrina, who'd latched on to the given name years before, in grade school, spits it out of her mouth at every opportunity. The tip of the pirate blade touches your stomach, and Marie scowls for a second as she pushes it and Katrina away.

Two stalls sit inside the cinder blocks painted wintergreen, a long horizontal mirror rests above the scuffed sinks, and a full-length mirror hangs to the left of it. The fluorescent bars beam chalky white light that flickers and gives the impression of a strobe at a disco party that's been all the rage for the past few years in North Carolina, a decade after it was all the fashion everywhere else.

Marie cuts you off. "You didn't say a word as long as I was helping you, Katrina." She fluffs the capped sleeves, then scratches her head through the scarecrow hat. "Besides, you got first pick, and you changed your mind twice."

Someone bangs on the door again, and a wave of hot blood rushes to your own face. You have a name of your own for Katrina; you try not to use it, but cannot help yourself. "Why did you lock the door, Catty?"

"Hey!" The voice is louder, as if hands are cupped over the mouth to form a bullhorn. "Other people need to use the bathroom."

"Use the boys' room," Marie calls out. "Marco was the only one in there, and he's outside helping set up now."

You look over at Marie. "He's spiking the punch, isn't he?"

Marie laughs. "He's trying to celebrate our birthdays a little early."

Marie's birthday is three days after yours. "As long as he doesn't get detention," you say.

"Well, I'm not going to say anything," Katrina says, sucking in her stomach and pursing her lips in front of the mirror. "Don't you say anything either, Diamond."

The banging on the door is more insistent now. "There are boys in there," the voice says again. "I can't hold it forever."

"Okay, okay," Marie says, stepping past Katrina and unlocking the stainless steel bolt, "keep your pants on."

Katrina, a slender pirate in Marco's costume, glares with her one unpatched eye at the next wave of girls entering the bathroom.

"This isn't your dressing room, you know," says April Stewart, whose parents came down from Richmond today, for a barbeque and the show that is playing at the local theater, a low-budget production of *The Phantom of the Opera*. April was living with her grandmother until her parents worked out the details of their separation.

"I didn't say it was," Katrina says. She runs her tongue over her teeth and then bares an artificial smile. "Is there lipstick where there shouldn't be?"

You look over Katrina and really see her for the first time in years: the tresses, the eyes that could be the sky at dusk, the freckled skin that seems to glow. Her mouth, usually a straight line compacted into a shape of disapproval and disappointment, is fire-engine red with lipstick.

You dig your whittled nails into the palms of your hands as you breathe in to steady yourself. "Why so particular today, Catty?"

"Why do you care, Diamond?"

April Stewart snickers, pulls out a coarse paper towel from the metal dispenser, and wipes her hands. She turns on her two-inch heels and leaves.

You step closer to the sink and look into the mirror, take a second to dab concealer under your eyes. You grimace at the lopsided pigtails and take out the left one to do over again.

Katrina laughs aloud. "Mess."

"Only because you've got one good eye," Marie calls out, her words as quick as a car salesman's.

You are grateful that Marie is there, but wish that once, just once, Marie would tell Katrina to shut up. You rearrange the bows, and step back as an unknown girl slips by her to wash her hands.

"Help me," Marie says. "I need another hand with Katrina's sash." The tinfoil sword dangles by a safety pin, and Marie tries to force the sash back in place. "You're too tall in those boots, take them off for a minute."

You smile at Marie and wait until Katrina pulls off the black galoshes. You hold the sash in place while Marie closes the gap with a second safety pin. Katrina fidgets, and you step on her bare feet with your ruby slippers, which are really just covers for your cheap tennis shoes. "I'm sorry, Catty," you say, and duck your head in shame.

"No, you're not." Katrina yelps in pain. "You just want to keep Marco all to yourself."

"Hold still," Marie commands, and all of the girls in the bathroom go silent. "Why any of you want my brother is beyond me."

Marco isn't the most handsome or the most athletic. But he is the most interesting: the object of his attention basks in a certain sunlight that soaks the skin and warms the soul.

"She only wants him because he doesn't pay attention to her," you say as if Katrina weren't in front of you, blue eye unblinking. "Katrina is always looking for the next new thing." She's held hands with every boy in school who's even said hello. Now she wants a boy who thinks she is invisible.

"It's better than being a tease, Heera," Katrina says. "You've been leading him on for almost a year."

You open her mouth to argue but Marie beats her hand against the tinfoil sword. "I've known you since preschool, Katrina. So I can tell you what I'm about to say . . ."

Katrina shoots deadeye toward Marie. "Really? You're taking her side? You know I've always loved Marco . . ."

"Until somebody else comes along, and somebody always comes along." Marie rolls her eyes. "Marco needs a girl who understands him."

"Save it, Marie," you say, stinging from the fact that Katrina has more history with the Grimaldi family, is invited to their Sunday dinners, talks to Marco whenever she pleases. "There's no boy in the world worth fighting over. If Katrina thinks she can capture Marco in that outfit, well, good luck to her."

Katrina says sweetly, "Did Marco choose Blackbeard after all? He was talking about it when I came over yesterday."

Your heart sinks like a ship anchor straight to your stomach as you remember Marco singing "Yo Ho! A Pirate's Life for Me" earlier in the week.

Marie grins, biting down on the third safety pin with her front teeth. She spits the pin into her outstretched palm. "Nope. He changed his mind before we left the house this afternoon."

You adjust the sword so that it hangs perfectly. "Oh?"

"The Tin Man."

It is your turn to smile but you hide it gracefully by pretending to yawn. "I'm not worried, Catty," you say. "Go for it."

"I don't need your permission," Katrina says. "Will you please stop calling me that?" She throws on the black rain boots and stomps out of the girls' room.

"I thought she'd never leave," says an unfamiliar girl at the sink.

"She's always like that now, especially since Chase went away to college this fall," says another girl, coming out of the stall, a white sheet pinned smartly into a toga. Louise Skinner. Her father manages the movie theater complex and she sits at the ticket window with her older sister every Saturday and notices everything. "You should see her in history, she's practically crawling over Mr. Cleveland when she thinks no one is looking."

"Eww," says the girl at the sink, smoothing an eyebrow with her fingers. "He's a teacher's aide."

You think of Mr. Cleveland's corny jokes, how he sometimes refers to himself as Mr. Ohio.

"He's not that cute either," Louise says.

"Enough," Marie says. Once more, the room quiets down. "We don't have any idea what's going on with her, or with anyone else. We shouldn't judge."

You roll your eyes. "That's pretty deep," you say. But you know Marie's right.

"Marco says that all of the time now, " Marie says, tossing back her head, a few golden strands of hay shaking free and falling to the ground. "He's safe from Katrina as long as I'm alive. Fifty years at least."

You grin. "2037," you say. "People will be living on the moon by then."

"Maybe Marco," Marie says. "His head is already in the stars."

You and Marie have just stopped skipping hand in hand to your off-key third rendition of "We're Off to See the Wizard" when you see them. Marco and Katrina, standing eye to eye thanks to Chase's boots. They are in front of the carnival cutouts, smiling at each other, arms encircling each other's waists.

"Just get one of us together before we put our faces through," Katrina says, her voice higher pitched than usual. Her skin is radiant.

The photographer shoos them to the side. "Strange to stand in front of the stand-ins," he says, patting his comb-over, the strands of which are the color of rawhide and the consistency of horsehair. "Position yourself by the bales of hay, and then I'll shoot," he says.

Marco obliges, taking Katrina by the hand and then with a flourish twirling her into a dip. The photographer laughs in delight and you hear the click of the camera shutter. They are skeletal bride and groom, grinning, their faces in place of sugar skulls. Marie uses her elbow to jab for attention. "You should be up there with him," she says, "It's your birthday."

You shiver a little in the weakening sun. The screams from the rickety roller coaster passengers echo in your chest and sudden valleys form at the base of your abdomen.

Marie links her arm through yours. When the next couple walks toward the cutout, Marie asks, "Marco, can I borrow the pirate bride for a second?"

Katrina blushes, and comes over. Marie adjusts the hay in her stomach and asks the photographer, "Can you take two pictures for us please?"

The photographer's smile is genuine. "For you, yes. That's the best Scarecrow I've seen in years," he says. "Who did your face?"

"My friend, Dorothy Gale, from Kansas," Marie answers, her hair peeking out of the bottom of her scarecrow hat.

Marie stands in between you and Katrina and commands, "Be nice." She shames you both with her eyes, prodding you to smile for the camera and feign love. "Get closer," she says more than once, each time the sparkle fading a little more from her skin, and steel entering her tone. You and Katrina are careful to put your arms around Marie in the middle without touching each other, while Marco holds up the oilcan, ostensibly filled with vodka.

The second photo takes longer. Katrina grabs Marco's hand and refuses to let go.

"It's just the folks from *The Wizard of Oz* in this one, sweetheart," the photographer says, endearments sugarcoating the annoyance in his voice.

Louise Skinner walks by with the unfamiliar girl from the bathroom sink, and whispers loudly, "Well, if Katrina wants it be in it so bad, why doesn't she turn around and hide her face?"

You look at Louise and shake your head slightly.

Louise snorts. "Those pants are something else. From the back she looks like a cowardly lion."

As cheerful music emanates from the direction of the Ferris wheel, you burst into laughter. The photographer freezes this moment for eternity: Marie's eyes round with amusement, Katrina smiling to hide the hurt, and Marco frowning at the cheapness of the joke. Only you know you are laughing in relief that Katrina chose the pirate costume.

The hayride is the best part of the fall carnival. A long spin around the Merrick's commercial farm that surrounds the Theater Center, the grounds all done up for Halloween the next day, scores of scarecrows positioned as sentries, black and orange balloons clustered along the mock lamps. Marco sits near the helm, the oilcan in his lap, Katrina on one side and the driver on the other. He turns his head back to see you and Marie pointing and laughing at the scarecrows. "What do you think? Not bad, huh?"

Marie shouts out, "Best time ever."

"Day's not over yet," you say to Marie. "Don't forget my birthday party tomorrow." Your mother and father relented after Marie said, "What do you mean there's no cake? Everyone has to have cake on her birthday! Three layers! Chocolate! Candles! Ice cream on the side!" Ma agreed to serve cake along with the traditional eight course Indian fare she cooks when company is coming, especially from out of town. Food is how your parents demonstrate love. There are enough of your mother's friends coming for dinner that you don't know well or at all. You should be more upset that strangers are to outnumber friends—but you don't care. Marie is invited and for once, this is more than enough.

&

Katrina has too much spiked fruit punch and falls into a stupor by the side of the makeshift tent where carnival games are being played. The prizes are hard to win, those larger-than-life Bengal tigers and giant smiling bears. You leave empty-handed. Marco has not touched the punch since he drank the first serving, content to watch others drink and encouraging them to refill their small plastic cups. You and Marie share one cup.

Halfway toward finishing, Marie says, "I don't know about you but this makes me sick to my stomach."

You toss the cup and its contents into the open garbage bin and help Marie to a foldout chair by the corn-dog stand. In the distance, Katrina is wobbling toward the Ferris wheel, with Marco as her crutch. "Lions and tigers and bears, oh my," you say.

Marie coughs a little. "Don't make me laugh," she says. "It makes my stomach hurt."

Katrina's father arrives just before the principal thanks everyone for coming and asks each participant to pick up three pieces of the trash strewn on the ground before exiting. Her father is a big and tall man, the opposite of Baba. Her father is here at the festival to pick up his daughter, unlike Baba who no doubt is dozing on the sofa, chicken curry and rice expanding in his stomach. You wish Katrina's dad had dressed in Viking attire to complement his flame-red beard and his one thick eyebrow. Marie stands up, hustles Katrina to the beverage area, and pours some black coffee into a white Styrofoam cup. "Drink this," she urges Katrina. "You'll wake up and stop smelling sickly sweet like the punch."

You walk back toward the bathrooms and the parking areas in silence, the ambient noise of high school girls chattering grows louder, competing with crickets and the light wind rustling tree branches dense with leaves the color of a blaze. "It's already too dark to walk to the other lot," Katrina's father says. "Stay here and I'll bring the car around."

Marco stops. "That's all right, sir, we won't be needing a ride."

"You're not serious?" Katrina stares at Marco. "It's so dark already. We have enough room, even Heera."

You look at your friends, and at Katrina. "That's kind of you."

Her father shakes his head. "I brought the coupe," he says. "Bucket seats."

"Go ahead," you say. "I'll be fine by myself."

Marco and Marie exchange a look, shake their heads in unison.

"You weren't going to walk Heera all the way home, were you?" Katrina asks. "That's four miles at least."

Marie points. "We just have to make it to Merrick's Convenience. She can change, and my mom is meeting us there, to drive us home." A scant mile down the two-way road.

Her father shrugs a little. "We can try to squeeze in, for the last mile."

Marco smiles in the ever-increasing dark. "The walk will do us good, sir."

"Maybe we could all walk to the convenience store, Dad," Katrina says. "And you could follow behind and pick me up from there."

Her father shakes Marco's hand and waves to the girls. "Come on, Katrina, that's not convenient. Your mother has already left for dinner at the neighbors' house."

Katrina walks backwards all the way to her father's car, her eyes blinking tears, her mouth twisted into an exaggerated frown.

Exits

LATER, AT THE HOSPITAL, YOU WILL REMEMBER HOW A CAR-
ton of spoiled milk and Marco's perfect aim have in fact, saved
your life—but not Marie's.

You and Marco and Marie skip hop walk from Merrick's Farm,
arms locking like the Three Musketeers—cars whizzing past you
as other festivalgoers' parents or older brothers are giving rides
home. Two people from school, you believe the Butler twins,
honk. Another altogether unfamiliar boy sticks his head out of
his father's metallic green Nova and yells, "Are you crazy? Get off
the road."

You remove your arm from the human chain link as Marco
pushes his sister closer to the ditch running by the road shoulder.

Marie pushes back a little, in jest. "Don't worry so much," she
says. "Just walk faster."

Marco shakes his head as the stars fill in the night sky. "Why
don't we walk single file?"

Marie salutes Marco. "Yes sir," she says. To you: "You walk
ahead, lead the way."

You listen, you walk briskly, with purpose, toward the four-
way stop in the distance.

After a minute Marco calls out, "Hey, you're leaving us behind."

Garbage is strewn along the roadside. Marco picks up a half-empty carton of milk and leaves his sister. He jogs a few steps ahead, a Tin Man on the move, and throws the carton at your feet, milk splashing your ankles. You stoop to pick up the carton. As you straighten your back and wind up to throw, Marie stands alone on the lane, laughing loudly. Marco gains speed toward you to affect your aim.

Headlights enter the road, synchronized yellow spheres that drift back and forth between opposing lanes.

The sound of car tires screeching.

You drop the carton. The smile freezes on Marco's face.

Marco turns in time as you both watch his sister take brief flight and crumple like a soda can.

Your throat and lungs hurt from the air being forced out, from the screams you hear yourself make. The woman in the passenger's seat screams too and covers her eyes with her hands.

Then stillness. Then chaos.

You and Marco run toward Marie, screaming and shouting, and then you lock eyes, briefly, with the driver. It is Mr. Thompson, the banker, the ex–school board member; you have seen his face on posters the last time he went up for reelection. He lurches forward in his seat for a moment, touching something below the steering column and then tries to turn off the radio, but cannot shut off the station entirely. Elvis croons "Love Me Tender."

You try to speak but you hear yourself moan. Your mind echoes *No No No No No No* until it is the only word you can hear, it is the only word you know.

Every sound is amplified. Mr. Thompson stumbles out of his seat and staggers toward Marco, at Marie's side not far from the car. Marco's hands cradle his sister's head. He calls her name, telling her to hang on, telling her that she'll be all right. You drop to your knees and wipe Marie's tears, her face paint streaks and smudges. You hold her hand and watch her look up at her brother's face covered in silver paint, his funnel hat askew, his chest heaving. You count the number of breaths Marie takes, seventeen in all, shallow, raspy, before blood begins to trickle out of the corner of her mouth.

As if by magic, an ambulance appears from the fire station across from Merrick's, medics telling you step aside, taking care when lifting Marie onto the stretcher.

The policeman with a pasty face and a mustache yells at Marco when he first pulls up in his squad car and parks crooked, blocking traffic. "What are you doing with her?"

Mrs. Thompson, whose younger brother owns the convenience store, speaks up. "Howard, that girl is his sister."

Howard's partner briefly focuses his flashlight into the Thompsons' Cutlass, the beam lingering near the brake and gas pedals, and then throws his arm around Mr. Thompson, steering him away from where the medics work to load Marie into the ambulance and rush her to the emergency room. Marco insists on accompanying Marie; the lights from police car and ambulance strobe over his face.

The medics load the stretcher gingerly and you see Howard's partner lean over the older man. You step closer, conscious of Marie's blood and makeup on your blue dress, on your fingers. The unmistakable odor of rum wafting through the night air.

"He's been drinking," Marco says, though he is far away from the driver, his eyes firmly fixed on Marie's paling face. He sits across from her and you know this moment will be imprinted in your brain forever.

We've all been drinking, you think. All drinking but only Mr. Thompson driving.

"We'll worry about that later," the officer says, and shuts the door to the ambulance. The siren sounds and the vehicle speeds away.

Somewhere inside you know these people will never worry about it again.

Mrs. Thompson gets out of the car and says to you, "My dear, let Officer Howard take you home."

You register the kindness in her voice but you cannot match it. "No," you say, "I have to go to the hospital."

She shakes her head. "Dear girl, they won't let you see her," Mrs. Thompson says. "You're not family."

"I have to go," you repeat.

Mrs. Thompson walks back to the Cutlass, Marie's blood a birthmark on the body of the road, and sits down in her seat, door still open, pulls down the sun visor and looks at herself in the tiny mirror. She reaches for her purse—takes out a tube of lipstick and tries to apply it. Her hands tremble and the lower lip is overdone, lipstick bleeding to the space just above the chin. "Hell's bells," she says, no luster in her voice.

Officer Mark walks to the other side of the patrol car and tells the drivers of the three or maybe four cars waiting to make a U-turn and go back. You glance at the front seat of the first car but don't see any familiar faces.

"Let's get you home, Miss Lacey," Officer Howard says. "Officer Mark will see Mr. Thompson to the door."

"Let's take the girl to the hospital, then," Mrs. Thompson says. "I don't want anything happening to her too, trying to get home."

Officer Howard looks you over the way Mr. Richard used to before Marie brought you PE gear.

You do not want to be alone with this man. "That's all right," you say. "I'll just walk."

"Are you crazy, girl?" Mrs. Thompson asks.

"Don't say another word!" Mr. Thompson's voice rings out like he is reading the morning announcements over a loudspeaker at your high school.

In the end, Mrs. Thompson gets Officer Mark to call a cab on the police radio, pulls money out of her purse, and places it between the fingers of your curled hand. You keep your eyes tightly closed during the drive to the emergency room. All you see is red. Although the cab driver only charges seven dollars, you hand over the fifty-dollar bill.

"I don't want the change," you say, not recognizing your own voice.

Carrying the one

OFFICIALLY HE IS MARCO AND YOU ARE HEERA. Your name represents a series of long unpronounceable expectations from a place across the globe that you never belonged to directly, but somehow the hooks are still there. Your name also represents what the good people of North Carolina want to see when they look at someone who looks like you, someone who looks so unlike them: a girl who is respectful and obedient, a girl who knows her place in their world, a girl who is invisible. In this way, the two worlds exist like an eternal syzygy.

Then the accident happens, the "not-accident," as Marco begins to say from the moment you arrive at the hospital still wearing a Dorothy costume stained with his sister's blood. You take turns, demanding to know where Marie is, how she is, what the doctors are doing to help her. Your questions echo down the hall and none of the hurrying bodies behind the nurses' station stop to answer.

Your parents and the Grimaldi parents arrive: your mother and Mr. Grimaldi spend an extra minute clasping hands, staring into each other's eyes, volumes unspoken.

"I'm so sorry, Rob," Ma says, finally. "This is more than one person should ever have to bear."

Mr. Grimaldi's face puckers into a silent wail.

A nurse comes into the waiting area and takes Mr. Grimaldi away.

Even your stoic father flinches in his vinyl seat when he hears Mrs. Grimaldi's screams. You put your hands over your ears, you stare at the double doors that lead to the operating rooms, you notice that it's one minute past midnight when they officially declare Marie dead. Your birthday. October 31. She is 17 years and 362 days old at the time of her death. The emergency room is very brightly lit; your eyes bounce between the white walls and the doctors' white coats and the white sheets on the stretchers. All the whiteness blinds, disorients. For a moment you forget why you are there.

Then you watch Marco transform into someone dangerous, someone unpredictable, someone who throws chairs in the waiting room, someone who curses and curses, someone who looks into your face but looks right through you, someone who accuses Mr. Thompson of drunk driving, someone who shouts "this was no accident" tens of times until it becomes "not-accident," someone who stares down Officers Mark and Howard when they respond to a call from the emergency room nurse.

You both change for good in those hours just after Marie dies.

You become the glassy hard brilliance of a diamond, dry-eyed and stoic, even after Ma insists you go home.

"The Grimaldis are not part of our family, Heera," she says. Her voice is firm but kind, her hands stroking the back of your costume. "Sona, it's time to leave."

At first, you say nothing.

Minutes crawl by, the second hand on the wall clock ticks continuously. You click your heels three times every five seconds until Ma puts a hand on your leg and asks you to stop. Machines beep behind nearby curtains, nurses speak into a microphone and read off colors and numbers, coded messages about the condition of other patients.

The paramedics bring in an older woman, a clear mask covering her nose and mouth, oxygen keeping her alive.

Then your father stands up, car keys in hand, sadness newly stamped on his face.

You say, "No, they are my family." You stretch out your hand and name each finger: Baba, Ma, you, Marie, Marco.

Baba sits back down, stares at nothing and everything and then at you. "The loss of your friend will stay with you for a very long time," he says, his Bengali yielding. "You need to rest."

You shake your head. "I need to stay here."

He shakes his head in return.

Your mother exhales, removes her hand from your back. She kneels in front of you. "They need their privacy, Heera, and we need ours."

Every day is the day of the dead

MONDAY. YOUR FATHER WAKES YOU GENTLY, WHISPERS the time, doesn't turn on the overhead light. Ma and Baba insist you go to school, as if nothing has happened, as if the world has not changed, as if your heart weren't irrevocably broken. You know every day from now on will be the day of the dead.

"You'll be glad later," Ma says, taking something out of the fridge and wrapping it in tinfoil.

"A person can only walk when he places one foot in front of the other," Baba says. "My father said that to me many times when life turned left instead of right."

You want to scream, but you don't have the energy.

You leave the house clutching the paper bag with your lunch inside. Baba tries to speak with you, he tries to tell you about his childhood friend who drowned in the sixth grade, but you look out the window and count the number of mailboxes you pass. There is congestion on the usual route, so he drives through the neighborhoods surrounding the school. You count twenty ugly mailboxes, six red flags standing at attention. As soon as he drives away from the horseshoe-shaped drop-off zone in front of the school, you toss the lunch bag into the nearest garbage can.

*

You are surprised to see Marco there, wearing a black T-shirt and dirty jeans, leaving the school office. You both stand in front of the guidance department, the door ajar. Gauzy curtains diffuse the sunshine but you can still see dust beginning to settle over the table, the droop of the banana leaf plant in the corner, a strand of cobweb hanging from the vent cover on the ceiling. "Why are you here?" you ask by way of greeting.

He snorts, and the noise echoes down the hallway. "The priest thinks that any semblance of normalcy will hasten healing."

You try not to frown but fail. "What?"

He runs his hands through his hair, his eyes looking ahead as though you weren't standing before him. "Nobody wanted me around when they discussed the . . . funeral arrangements."

Everyone keeps their distance from you both as the bell rings and people spill into the hallways. April Stewart sees you on her way to French but skirts by, wearing her grief plainly, with trembling lips and wet eyes.

Katrina is nowhere to be found.

The first time Marco says it, Crash, none of the students in third period laugh.

Roll call.

World History.

Mr. Cleveland goes down the list alphabetically. "Gaines?"

Michael answers, "Here."

"Grimaldi?"

"My name is Crash now," he says quietly.

A collective gasp and shudder. Downturned mouths; one girl in the back begins weeping.

Mr. Cleveland's eyes widen.

You turn around in your seat to try to catch Marco's eye, but he stares at the blackboard, today's date written in cursive.

భ్

You insist on accompanying him to his house during lunch. "Let's walk," you say.

At first he shakes his head.

You grab his hand. "Crash," you say. "It's me."

He looks at you, his eyes red and defeated and angry. "Who are you?"

You inhale. "Dia."

He doesn't miss a beat. Recognition returns. "My diamond girl," he says, "for the day of the dead."

You exhale. "I'll walk you home."

And he doesn't object.

You hold on to his arm like a drowning girl hangs on to a life preserver.

The second time he says it is after school, to his mother, who asks him for a glass of water from the far end of the sectional where she is curled into a ball. The Grimaldi parents scream at each other. They cannot bear to be in Marie's room, they cannot bear to be out of Marie's room. You run upstairs two steps at a time. Everything stationary: rejected clothes strewn on the floor; a glass of water, half drunk, on the dresser; her homework atop an unmade bed, her hot-pink comforter bunched up, like an accordion, against the wall. You walk downstairs slowly.

Mr. Grimaldi suggests they should plan to empty Marie's room when the time is right, and Mrs. Grimaldi says that it is now a shrine, that it will forever be a shrine, that it will remain as their only daughter left it.

Mr. Grimaldi runs his hands through his hair, and then covers his face with them.

"I'm Crash now, Mom," he says, handing her a plastic glass of water.

She sits up, takes the glass, and flings the tepid liquid into his face.

Mr. Grimaldi quietly tells her to stop.

You want to grab Crash's hand and drag him away. Instead you run to the kitchen and grab paper towels.

You try to mop up the water but Mrs. Grimaldi snatches the paper towels from you and flings them at Crash.

The telephone rings and Mr. Grimaldi rushes to answer it in the study. He returns to the living room a few minutes later, his face flushed, streaked with tears. "Heera, your mother wants you home."

Fast

THE DAYS LEADING UP TO THE FUNERAL, CRASH COUGHS steadily.

First a sputter, then a persistent tickle at the back of the throat. Then a barking, whooping cough that you think is a cry for help. You ask Ma if Crash can spend the night in your guest bedroom, take a break from his parents' funeral planning and fights about Marie's room.

Baba answers with a resounding "No." Baba, who is always so conscious of what he eats and drinks, begins smoking again. After a ten-year gap, he ends up going through half a pack during the course of a single day.

You walk to the Grimaldi residence, watch neighbors bring over plates of cold fried chicken and green bean casserole. They bravely eat a bit, put much of it into the fridge. When you return home, you ask Ma to make the Grimaldi family something to eat, something better than greasy fried chicken and green beans cooked in what appears to be condensed mushroom soup.

She agrees but the kitchen remains dark, the stove's coils remain cool to the touch.

Your birthday party was canceled. There is a mountain of food to be consumed and yet your parents shovel everything into cardboard boxes and arrange for a donation to the local food bank.

You ask why.

"This is how we mourn in our culture," Ma says. "We fast."

❧

You stand in Crash's living room, his mother sits on the couch, takes the stuffing out of her throw pillow one small piece at a time, and tosses it all onto the carpet. His father once in a while runs down the hallway to the bathroom and vomits into the toilet, door ajar. You gently counsel your friend to sit down, to lie down, to rest, to sleep.

Crash stares at you and opens his mouth to speak but cannot.

Instead the doorbell rings, and he answers: Katrina and her father, bearing bouquets of gladioli, Marie's favorite; and a scrapbook of pictures from elementary school and shared camping trips.

It is the first time you've seen Katrina since the carnival: her cheeks are hollow. She embraces Crash for what seems an eternity, she buries her head in his neck. She glides right by you.

Mrs. Grimaldi allows Katrina to hug her.

Mrs. Grimaldi returns Katrina's smile.

You fight the urge to sob when your eyes begin to well.

"I think you should go home now," Mrs. Grimaldi says to you, her eyes lifeless.

Katrina and her father busy themselves by putting the flowers in a crystal vase, and Mr. Grimaldi's shoulders slump as he looks away.

Once again, Crash opens and closes his mouth without uttering a sound.

So you leave.

❧

At the beginning of the homily and funeral mass, it is daylight and you are bitterly cold, your hands stiff, arthritic. Crash looks put together in a way, showered and in a dark suit, but utterly devastated. Crash hacks away, mouth covered by cupped hands, not even trying to stop during the blessing and prayer at the end. You and your parents sit far from him, in a pew near the back of the church. Yet his coughs are so loud it as though he is next to you, and your elbows are touching. You want to get up, help, but Ma puts her hand on you and Baba gently shakes his head.

Mr. Grimaldi stands and tells him to leave the sanctuary for fresh air and water, walks him down the aisle and out the door. It occurs to you that he will never walk Marie down this same aisle, that she will remain seventeen forever, that she will never graduate from high school or college, that she will never go on a date or fall in love, that she will never marry or have children of her own, that she will not be there to share in your triumphs or commiserate in your disappointments, that her absence will be a deafening silence, that the silence will likely drive you mad. You stifle an urge to cough, like Crash. Katrina and her parents sit behind the Grimaldi grandparents, openly crying. From where you sit, you crane your neck to see Mrs. Grimaldi's profile, and it looks like her eyes are tightly shut.

Her husband returns, alone.

By the time the funeral is over, the light has changed. It is no longer the promise of morning but instead it is after noon and it is winter so the sun appears to descend faster, as if running away. Then you are at the gravesite, the air is chilly and the wind has picked up its pace, from slow dance to foxtrot.

At the burial, Katrina cries into the shoulder of her father, who stares impassively at the coffin. Katrina will not look at you and then briefly does: you realize that she blames you for this moment and all the moments that will come after this. She blames you for walking on the road with Marie. You know everyone blames the drunk driver, but as much as they can blame you for walking on the road in the newly minted evening, they will. People like order. You wonder if everyone blames you in the same way Katrina does.

Your breath flies out of your body as they lower the coffin. The tightness in your chest suffocates, you wonder if you will faint. You sense something and look behind you, past the shoulders of your parents, half expecting to see Crash in the distance. But it is only a crow, a murder of one.

Crash doesn't return home for days.

Lights

THE MOMENTS YOU ARE NOT WITH CRASH YOU SEE COCK-roaches, tens of them streaming in geometric formations across the floor in the kitchen in the evening just before dinner or along the hallway to your parents' bedroom in the mornings.

The moments you are not with Crash you detect a platoon of spiders descending from the dining room ceiling as the lettuce wilts in your salad, and your lunch remains intact.

The moments you do not see Crash you spy ants marching single file in the shower, and find yourself unable to step in and turn on the water.

You know you are the only one to see them, that you are alone in your grief. Your mind is a slideshow, even as you attempt sleep, one photograph rapidly dissolving into the next: you and Marie, arms crossed, refusing to eat scrambled eggs after your first grade class hatches downy chicks in a special incubator that spring; Marco knee-deep in the pond one summer later, helping the science camp teacher release the tadpoles back to their habitat; Marie fostering a pair of stray kittens, feeding them from tiny bottles and posting handmade signs around the neighborhood until they were adopted—all their efforts in the care and feeding of others, those who were helpless. Now all that love has vanished, though the pictures continuously loop inside you.

Your parents watch the television news, the pointed black hands of the clock in the kitchen, you.

Your parents try to make conversation, ask you about your studies, shoo you away from your usual chores, ask you to join them as they begin a new tradition, traipsing to the backyard in the evenings to look at the stars. They ask you to join on the suddenly frequent telephone calls they make to India.

"Just say hi," Baba says one Saturday morning, offering the green receiver. "It's your great-aunt."

But you walk past in a daze, unable to fake a smile or a cheery voice or answer their repetitive questions with the enthusiasm that's expected of you. You go outside with them once and point out Orion's Belt, three stars in a row, remember Marco's obsession with astronomy in the fifth grade and his giant constellation poster for the science fair, how you took turns lining up the hole punch, then threading the tiny white Christmas lights through the openings so he could have a prop for the audience to look at while he told stories about Queen Cassiopeia and Polaris and the Big Dipper. You barely make it back inside in time to vomit bile in the half bathroom by the kitchen. You scarcely choke down a half piece of toast, everything tastes bitter, you spy leftovers of Halloween candy in a melamine bowl, everything untouched.

"She's a little sad," Ma says once to the voice on the other end of the line. "You know, her friend."

You practice looking past them, and soon you are able to tune out their words.

You wish you could call Crash or go by and see him, tell him about the insects.

But he is not home. He is never home.

Your parents insist that you accompany them the next time the Bhoumicks invite them to dinner. They are the relatively new Bengali family to move to Raleigh, from Oklahoma City. Your mother holds up the red salwar kameez but you shake your head.

"I'll wear something black," you say. "For mourning."

Ma says no. "We don't wear black for those occasions."

But you don't own any Indian clothes that are white, the proper color for mourning. In the end you wear a salwar kameez that is midnight blue and plain. You leave the shiny scarf Ma gives you in the backseat of the car.

Auntie Bhoumick's hug is awkward but warm, and she pats your back as if you're a baby in need of burping. Despite Baba's protests over caffeine and tooth decay, Uncle Bhoumick procures for you a tall glass of cola, the ice cubes shifting and cracking in a fizzy sea. You are among the first to arrive, and the Bhoumicks' younger daughter, Anjuli, asks you to play with her: you follow her to the backyard, her daffodil-print dress flutters in the breeze, her two braids swing back and forth in unison. You spy the swing set and offer to push. "Higher, Heera Didi," she tells you in between giggles. "Higher!" The air is crisp and it is a relief to forget everything, even for a moment.

Later, as more guests arrive, you retreat.

Alone you sit in the kitchen and think of the last party you went to with Ma and Baba, at the Mukherjees' when Marie was very much alive. You sat alone in the kitchen that evening too, but you held a copy of *The Scarlet Letter* in your hand. You remember Anita Auntie, whose turn it was to host the following week, sneaking in, pen and cocktail napkin in hand, moving quickly in her simple black sari, her pageboy haircut flying behind her. You surprised her with a discreet cough, and she laughed; the two of you tasted the chicken butter masala ahead of everyone else, and Anita Auntie jotted down notes. You remember recounting the story to Marie at school the following Monday, and her offer to trade her ham sandwich for your chapati egg wraps.

The Bhoumicks' eldest daughter, Krishna, is home from boarding school in Maryland. She breezes in late, takes you into her darkroom in the basement. "I lost a good friend to a drunk driver last year," she says. A shadow of anguish passes over her face. "My baba gave me a camera. Therapy."

You look around, a giant bulletin board dominates the far wall, a Tulane University pennant tacked next to a homemade sign: GOALS!

"New Orleans, huh?"

"I can't wait to go there," Krishna says, her voice electric. "It's been my dream for such a long time."

You count six nature photographs pinned to the bulletin board. Your two favorites: the ocean foam looping just before its fall onto a beach, and an owl asleep in a tree, nestled into the trunk as it intersects with a thick branch.

"Where's this from?" You point the picture of the sea.

"Ocean City, Maryland," she says, a smile on her lips. "Near my school." She offers you her parents' telephone number, to talk, and the use of her darkroom. "Come back sometime soon."

You tell Baba about Krishna's darkroom.

Ma comes home with a camera the next day.

The day after that, you see Crash at school and tell him what Krishna said.

Soon, Crash and his new camera are inseparable.

You and Crash smile at each other, not every day, but still.

Before Krishna leaves for school again, you return to her house and develop a few: the winter sun spattering through the branches of the sycamore at the park; Baba holding up the broad pages of the newspaper, obscuring all of his body except for his thin hands; the worry lines around the corners of Ma's mouth when she believed she was alone, sitting by the window looking out to the street; the horizon on the first day after break begins, the sky bland but the clouds dark and hanging low.

Physical evidence of your grief.

Expectations

I THOUGHT I HEARD THE SLIDING GLASS DOOR," MA SAYS, HER back turned to you and Baba.

She washes red onions under the tap. The air smells of cilantro and ginger and garlic. "I don't hear an answer, Heera," she says. "My question was simple. Did you go out last night with Marco?"

Baba lowers the newspaper and drops his cigarette butt into the cereal bowl, which only has a thin residue of fat-free milk glazing the bottom. His eyes are like the pebbles in the garden, smooth and neutral and enduring through all of the elements.

You know you should confess, that you shouldn't lie, that you'll be caught later and the punishment will be so much worse than anything your mother, wielding a kitchen knife and peeling back a red onion, could do right now. "It's Dia," you say.

Your mother, dressed in a housecoat and apron, wipes her nose on the collar of the housecoat, her shoulders tremble as her weeping shakes her body, doesn't reply. No red onion is that strong.

"I haven't seen Crash, Ma." You look into your own bowl of cereal.

"I heard something outside," she insists.

"That was me, Ma." You gesture toward the PE shoes you left outside last night. "I was looking for my shoes, for school."

Your mother cries openly, as she uses the broad side of the knife to push the onions into the frying pan, the olive oil sizzling and spitting in the center. She quickly covers the onions with the lid of a bigger pan and dumps the knife and cutting board in the sink. "All I want is your honesty, Heera," she says, turning so that her back is up against the stainless steel lip.

"You have it, Ma," you say, attempting to match your father's eyes.

You ask yourself, why is Crash the only person you can bear to see now? Why is Crash's pain more important than anyone else's? And the answer is the same for both questions. Ready at the lips, instant: because he's all that's left of Marie, whose voice and face you remember each time you take a breath.

You ask yourself: why do you lie? You look over at Ma, and see her shoulders hunched. You answer your own question: to stem the tears from your mother's eyes, and for you to keep from running away for good. It is a poor and precarious status quo, but it is all you can manage.

Your father's gaze hardens.

The question returns: why do you lie? Because Crash makes you laugh. Because Crash sees you. Really sees you. And because he misses her too.

"All I want is your understanding," Ma says, walking toward you at the table. She picks up both bowls and takes them to the sink. "I am not American, I don't say I love you all of the time." She turns on the faucet, picks up a sponge, and begins scrubbing the cereal from the side of the bowl.

You try to remember the last time you heard her say it, and then you know: you've never heard her say it. "That's okay," you say.

"I don't have to say I love you, Heera," she says loudly to the cutting board she has picked up and begins washing. "I provide everything for you. I make dinner, I make breakfast, I pack your lunch. I buy you nice clothes."

Your father raises the newspaper again. "She doesn't like the food or the clothes," he says.

She coughs. "I take you to the beach."

Baba mumbles under his breath.

It's not enough, you want to say — not enough of a balm for the grief that pervades every waking moment and every breath. You cannot mention to her how bad it is, how Marie's absence is a black hole, sucking the life out of every effort. Marie's death has taken the shape of an abyss, Crash is the only tether, and he has stopped coming most days. Katrina scowls when she spots you in the hallways, and drops her eyes. She says nothing when the Kaminski brothers resume stretching your given name into a joke in the cafeteria. Then you blurt out, "I want to wear jeans to school, Ma." You taste shame in your throat as you realize that you don't care about the jeans themselves. What you really want is to disappear.

"That's why you lie to me and leave the house in the dark?" she asks. "I'm getting sick because of this."

You think of something smart to say. You consider telling the truth, that the only time you can think of Marie without seeing insects, without feeling faint, without wanting to lie down and die is when you're in the company of her brother, at a water tower, at a bus station, or behind Merrick's.

You recognize her tone, you have not heard it in years, it is the sound of defeat. Ma lived in a joint family for years growing up, all the cousins and all the aunts overrunning her sweet parents with their rules — she got married to get away from all of those rules. For a while she would say the name of the old neighborhood quickly. You thought it was a particular part of town that everyone knew, but it turns out that she was slurring her words together, that the memory of that place was so painful she would utter its name hurriedly. Karbala Tank Lane. Much later when you had started high school and went for two weeks over winter break, she had pointed to a shabby structure off a wide alley, second from the main street in Maniktala, in Goa Bagan, called Pearly Row. You saw the water tower for which the street is named, looming overhead, painted sage green.

You know you should have tried to memorize more of where she lived the first part of her life, but you didn't—taken instead with the cluster of neatly trimmed gardenia bushes in front of a gated house off Pearly Row. From the open window you could smell them. When you think of Kolkata, you always remember the smell of gardenia mixed in with the diesel from the public buses.

Baba was not much better that last time, driving past Bag Bajar, face frowning into a what his uncle had called a Bangla paanch, the number five in Bengali script. Someone in the taxi was begging Baba to return home, for good. You on the way to a wedding, some cousin of Baba's whom you hadn't seen since you were five and you had virtually no recollection of except that he had snuck you an extra sandesh when Ma wasn't looking.

"She is ill," your father says, behind the newspaper, snapping you from the memory. "Whatever has happened is finished now, for your mother's sake."

"What does that mean?" you ask, although you already know. Still the answer surprises you. The finality of it.

"Your mother needs help, Heera." He puts down the paper. "You will stop seeing him outside of school."

The cold that has lingered with Ma forever is a blood disorder, part of the diseases that make up myelodysplastic syndromes, he says. Her white cells are not operating the way they should. It has been caught early and can be treated, he says.

You look at Ma and Baba, and your heart plunges to the floor. The sadness that is stamped on Crash's face resides in your parents' eyes too.

⚬⚬⚬

Baba checks the Indian calendar pinned to the other side of the door to the study, the pages curling at the bottoms, a picture of the goddess Kali above the month, her eyes bulging, her tongue out and down to her blue-skinned chin. Bengali lunar calendar. He retrieves something from the shelf and carries it into the kitchen.

Baba pores over an old photo album on the anniversary of his mother's death. You remember her from years before, a kind woman in a white sari who fed you pineapple slices and told you she chose your name, her American granddaughter. You never met his father. He has been an orphan for years, thumbing through sepia photographs at the kitchen table, still life. Baba says their names, from his side and from Ma's side too. Their families' shared history a balm.

You think you can remember those many names, great-grandparents who migrated from a town named for a king, and then moved back to rural Bengal, their entire village in tow. The one who was a homeopathic doctor, the one who was a great cook. And the other great-grandparents on Ma's side, where they lived and how, before Partition eviscerated their lives and they were forced to move to Kolkata. You repeat them but they slip away, extinguishing like a flame at the end of a wick, the wax pooling as the candle melts.

You cannot hold anything but Marie lying on the ground and her labored breathing, and Marco, the lights from the ambulance as they moved counterclockwise over his face. And then Baba stops at a photo of her, his maternal aunt who was dead before he was even born. Bride, burned. Although outlawed in India, the practice of fatally injuring a daughter-in-law was not abandoned. Times changed all the time, he says, but people stayed exactly the same.

Ma drinks masala tea at the table, then stands over his shoulder to look. "Oh yes," she says, at the sari-clad girl's photo. "I remember what your mother said about her."

You get up and look too. The girl is long dead but it could be you. The girl in a sari standing in a rose garden. You could be twins, generations apart.

Baba says her name.

Khuku Roychowdhury.

You remember this name. Ma has told you about this name in recounting of family lore. The girl who died at the hands of her in-laws, the girl who died alone.

Khuku. Your great-aunt on your father's side. The eldest in a family supported by her father, the homeopathic doctor. Ma recounts what she knows and what she's learned. Baba pauses from poring over the photo album. A tear escapes one eye, leaves a wet line down to his chin.

Lithe Khuku hustling to get her mother what she wanted, beloved in a family with several sons and the elder of two daughters. Her younger sister was your grandmother, Rani. The youngest always rules the roost in any Bengali family, and she was the queen.

But Khuku was the shine in her parents' eyes, a charming girl with a light laugh and an even lighter touch. There was a handsome young Bengali boy in the next village and when she was in her teens, she was married to him. A few months later, she was dead.

She cooked one day and her mother-in-law caught the fifteen-year-old tasting a piece of the fried fish. Her mother-in-law forcibly dipped her hands into the cooking oil, to punish her for tasting. The hands became septic. She died a painful and horrible death and her parents and her brothers were kept from her in her final hours. She died alone and unavenged.

"The one brother of hers that was still living forty years later didn't know—he still didn't know," Ma murmurs.

You gape while Baba nods.

The males of the family were only ever told that an "illness" led to her death. The women of the world knew, with their stories and their looms and their knitting needles, and those brief moments after the lunches were made and everyone was on their backs napping for a few minutes in the noonday heat, the whispered stories that have been woven through the brain stems and rested under the eyelids of these many generations of women.

"I told your baba when his mother told me," Ma says. "I could not keep this history from him."

Baba weeps openly. Your stomach crawls as you think of Khuku's murder. A dowry death.

The husband didn't know what had happened either, Ma says. Her husband, who was a few years older than her, was away with his cousins the day Khuku fried fish, and as there was no telephone or mail courier or ambulance, he came home to find his new wife dead and his mother looking through a stack of letters from potential replacement brides.

He purportedly remarried four months later.

Ma says, "We don't know when she died, we don't know where they spread her ashes."

The story is over and Baba wipes his eyes with a handkerchief he produces from his pants pocket. Ma turns away.

You look out the window: the sun still shines down, the trees still sway in the breeze, nothing has changed, everything has changed. So much loss in the world, and still the world spins forward, stopping for no one.

The telephone rings. It is your great-uncle and his wife. True warmth in your parents' voices when the uncles and aunts call but there is a shift, steel under their pleasantries. Now that Ma is sick, you see the desire to return home to India flee their faces and they beg off. They do not disclose that Ma is ill. Instead, they use you as an excuse. They can't move back because of their American daughter. "How could we ask Heera to leave her home?" Ma says loudly into the receiver. You look out the window as you walk away, brown thrashers chant as they cluster in a nearby tree. It sounds like young voices answering *but you did but you did.* Today is not long after Marie has died, and for a single moment you want to run away and start over somewhere that Marie has never seen, but then the hurt comes in a rush.

Bargain

IT IS JUST LIKE CRASH TO NEVER WANT TO PAY, NOT FOR THE smokes he lifts from the glove box in his cousin's BMW, not for the sodas he walks out with from Mr. Merrick's convenience store, not for the dinners and dates that lead to sex he says he has with all of those girls who go to the private school just down the way.

An all-girls' school that has trellises for the ivy on those new buildings designed to look centuries old. Ivy clings to the lattice-work. You'd begged Baba to stop one afternoon on the way back from the grocery store so you could take a photo. Crash boasts how he spends the evenings and weekends at the girls' school.

"Why should I have to pay for anything?" Crash asks, his voice modulated but clearly amused. You are in front of the store, after Crash has helped himself to a two-liter bottle. Mr. Merrick has looked the other way, again, shuffling to the storage room in the back. Mrs. Thompson has left a standing order with her brother and his family: *Give the boy what he wants.*

Crash offers you a sip of root beer, but you cannot bear to consume anything from Merrick's anymore. You are thirsty, but you shake your head no. "Nothing is for free," you say. "Everyone has to pay eventually."

"We'll see," he says, but in a tone that says, *Not Me.*

"What's there to see?" you ask, pointing to the jug. "One day

soon all of your teeth will fall out and not too long after that"—
you glance down below his waist for a second—"other parts will
fall off too."

Crash laughs. His teeth are straight, pearly. "You are such
a prude, Dia, you can't even say it. Penis. You think my penis is
going to fall off."

Your face reddens and you are glad the sun has already sunk
below the horse barn in the distance. Your stomach rumbles but
you know you can't leave for home just yet, it is early still and you
don't want the questions or the inevitable lecture. You are supposed to be at the high school library, practicing with the speech
and debate team. It is your senior year.

It is Crash's senior year too.

Again.

You quit the speech and debate team but only Crash knows.
You have tried to live the life your parents want for you, but you
stray. If and when you see Crash it is during the week; you give
away your weekends to your family.

"Well, it might," you say. "Anyway, the tooth fairy doesn't
come for adult teeth." Sometimes you wish Crash would pursue
you the way he does the private school girls but then your hands
begin to shake and you know you are not ready for anything more
than friendship.

"Nah," Crash says, and he uses the empty bottle like a basket-
ball and makes a perfect free throw into the black mouth of the
open garbage can. "They're all virgins."

You laugh. "Right," you say. "And you believe everything they
say." An unfamiliar car passes the front of the store, honks at us,
and then its driver turns on the headlights.

"Nothing's on fire yet." He smiles.

"You're demented, Crash," you say. "If you spent half the time on your homework as you do on those girls, you'd be in honors rather than detention."

He picks up another bottle. "If you spent less time worrying about every little thing, you'd smile more and look less like Mother Hubbard."

"Who's she, again?"

He twists off the top. "A sour old bat from a nursery rhyme."

You shift your sleeve and look at your watch with its cracked face. It is winter but the only clue is that the sun sets more quickly, and darkness is a more consistent companion. Dark when you wake up and dark when you go to bed, the best part of the day spent indoors at desks, staring at incomprehensible formulas and theorems on the blackboards.

Crash has eyes everywhere on his body, it seems.

"Stop counting the seconds until you can leave," he says, dropping to his knees and opening the zippered pocket in the front of his backpack. He pulls out a key. "C'mon, I'll entertain you until your old man leaves to pick up your mom."

Your mother is sick, but still working at the library. Your father leaves every evening at five to fetch her from work, and then they walk a couple of loops inside the nearby mall, window-shop, stop for tea. You are supposed to come home right after debate practice, you are supposedly friends again with Katrina and sometimes stop at her house to study, plan for college admissions. None of this is true, but some days it buys you a few moments with Crash when he isn't off joyriding with friends, skipping school. Today, however, you are not in the mood to listen to his list of conquests.

Your eyes train on Crash, with each second the darkness turns his face into a silhouette. "How do you know what I'm waiting for?"

"I'm not dumb," he says. "I've had a year to figure it all out." He puts the pack on his shoulders and tightens the strap.

"We have an agreement . . ." you say.

"Yeah, yeah," Crash answers. "I'm not asking any questions. Just follow me."

You walk away from Merrick's store and the road, on a path that has been cleared by the wheels of kids' bikes over the years, past the holding pond, with the moon on its back, an empty cradle, to guide you. You both walk in the tall grass behind the painted white fences and iron gates, and onto a narrow slip of concrete between a cluster of office complexes and cars parked tightly next to the curb. Somewhere in the complex a custodian has turned up a soap opera on the radio in what sounds like Hindi besieged by broken English. You keep walking until the businesses drop off and the neighborhoods spring up, the lanes of the roads widen, trees appear on the medians.

The front door has a new deadbolt and Crash has to shake the key inside the lock and coax it to open. You say nothing, dreading where you are now and dreading the moment you have to go home and pretend to be happy in the way your parents think you ought to be.

"Stop thinking about it," he says, and then the door gives way and he steps inside, flicks the light switch with his forearm. "Come in."

You hesitate, uncertain of what you will see and whether you even want to see. It is not the arrangement you and Crash have agreed to, since you first gave your word to your parents after Marie's funeral. All of the play between you and Crash is done outdoors, in full view of anyone who cares to watch. But no one cares, and no one really ever notices you. You have a standing invitation the first and middle of every month: you are supposed to meet behind Merrick's for a drink, or just to catch up. Lately, he is behind the wheel of his cousin's car, driving alongside you, telling you how sorry he is, that something has come up; then speeding off. In school, you barely acknowledge each other. "Crash, what if your mother comes home?"

He shrugs and then turns and stretches out his hand—"You should see the place now. It's different."

"It's been a while," you say. You count the months. It's been more than a year since you were last inside his living room, almost fourteen months since Marie died.

You take his hand. His palm is dry but you are both trembling—just a little, a series of small tremors beneath the surface. Barely felt but felt nonetheless. You step inside the threshold and look around. You drop each other's hands but stand side by side and then walk in step to all of your once familiar locations. The walls are now a freshly painted ecru, and all of the dolls and knick-knacks from Greece and Nepal and the Philippines are in a large glass cabinet, the brass key shining in its keyhole, the wood paneling from the den removed and the walls covered with old family photos, photos of Marco as a baby, and of his cousins and uncles, and of his grandmother, judging from the fade of time, not long after she'd arrived in the United States as a bride, the Golden Gate Bridge behind her, a rusting sentry at the end of a long day. A memorial of Marie's framed baby photos next to the bay window. You exhale and catch Crash's gaze.

"Wait until you see the bathroom, Dia."

But you don't want to see the bathroom, or the kitchen, you don't want to point out to Crash what you know he could plainly see for himself, that no amount of remodeling would ever conjure a different past.

"What about her room?" you find yourself asking aloud.

"Dad lost." Crash grunts. "Mom won't let anyone in there."

The paint smells new still, as though the house was remodeled the day before. There is a faint patina of dust from the new hardwood floors covering the countertop and the oversized mahogany table with pearl inlay, no doubt a purchase from the Asian furniture market where your own mother had found hers years before. You look at a shoe rack and find only women's pumps.

"Where is your dad?" You remember him escorting his son out of the church on the day of Marie's funeral. You remember his face: he lost both of his Italian twins in a single moment.

"He's sleeping at the office now," Crash says, his tone indifferent. "Sometimes he goes to his sister's house."

You try not to gasp. "Why?"

"He made the mistake of making Marie's bed." Crash's eyes ablaze. "Now he has to sleep at my aunt's."

You try not to put your hand over your own mouth. "I need to go home," you say. "I can't be late and we can't be together in this house."

Crash points vaguely in the direction of the clock with its Roman numerals on the far wall. "Don't call that place home, Dia," he says.

"Ditto." You cross your arms as you stride toward the foyer where you have left your things. You are bending down to lift your bag when the door opens and a woman enters, her heels click-clacking cheerily, a figure behind her. "Marco, look who I found—" Mrs. Grimaldi stops dead and looks you over as if you're a stranger breaking in. Anger ripples over her face and she glares briefly at Crash.

You stand tall, your bag a baby cradled in your arms, and look back at the woman who could have been your mother-in-law in one life, but never in this one.

F-stops

IN THE DREAM, YOU SIT IN A CLASS CROWDED WITH STUDENTS. You discuss photography, f-stops, aperture, acute and obtuse angles. You wear a sweatshirt the color of the university that has accepted you for admission. Royal blue sky, a lion for a mascot. A full scholarship. A big city far enough from your parents that you won't feel watched all of the time. The city of your birth. In the dream, you open the workbook and gasp: your photograph of the reclining Buddha serves as a model of composition and color, and Crash's deadline photos from the riots overseas are mentioned as examples of courage under fire.

Your parents are so proud. They make photocopies of the pages of the textbook, they wait in line at the post office for hours and mail off copies to relatives in India. In the dream, your parents take you shopping to pick out furniture and bedding for your college dormitory. It is an alternate life where Marie is still alive, and you and she will be roommates. The two of you take the train all the way to New York City, and push open the window next to your seat. You thrust your hand out. The wind is balmy on your skin, the sun is shining, and you are waving goodbye.

When you awaken, your letter is opened and waiting for you at the kitchen table, next to a brand-new transistor radio with a red bow on top and an IOU in Baba's careful script on notebook paper for a trip to the beach. The university that you have dreamt of has congratulated you, accepted you, and plans to welcome you next fall. A partial scholarship. You read and reread your acceptance letter, smile broadly, breathe the morning air wafting in from the sliding glass door, mingling with the fried eggs untouched on your parents' plates.

Neither Ma nor Baba smiles in return.

Their silence is vociferous.

Your heart accelerates. Finally you ask, "Aren't you happy for me?"

Ma nods. "Very proud."

Baba clears this throat. "You mother has had to stop working. She will need further treatment."

You look at Ma, who is trying not to cry. "What are you saying?"

Baba explains that the money they have saved for college is needed for Ma's treatment. The blood disorder has gained strength. Complications with medicine allergies. "There's a clinic in New York," he says.

You look from one sad face to the other and back again.

Ma coughs, and it sounds like a freight train barreling through the night. "She has to go to college," Ma says, after catching her breath.

Baba nods. "There's still a way for us all to be there."

Girl, missing

YOU LEARN IN REVERSE ORDER.

First you drive by the new billboard on Glenwood Avenue. Krishna's high school yearbook face smiling down on you with the word MISSING in bold red letters above her head and an 800 number just below the neckline of her sweetheart blouse. A collective gasp, and Ma calls out god's name. Baba swerves in his lane for a few seconds before righting the wheel. The hard stop at the next traffic light as it turns yellow, and all three of you turning your heads back to look again.

Krishna.

Missing for a week, according to the billboard.

You think about your last interaction with her, several weeks before, in the darkroom, her easy laugh, her excitement about Tulane and spending her college years in New Orleans, far from North Carolina, and far from Oklahoma where she grew up and where her friend was killed by a drunk driver. You wonder how all this happened. Krishna was only supposed to be at home for a few days, a break. You reduce your fears to monosyllabic answers as Baba questions you from the driver's seat:

> Q: *Do you know anything about this?*
> A: *No.*
> Q: *Are you sure she's missing?*

A: Yes.

Q: Do you know her friends?

A: No.

Q: How are you certain that she's missing?

A:

You have no answer. You know Baba is skeptical because his only child is a part-time thief.

You lock eyes with Baba in the rearview mirror. Both fear and anger dwell in his gaze.

When you arrive home, your mother places a series of phone calls, to the 800 number, to the local police, to some mutual friends in the Bengali community. She recounts the puzzle pieces she's gleaned: Krishna home for a break, borrows the family sedan to drive to a specialty store in Greensboro for darkroom supplies. She doesn't return. Later that evening, her car found by the police on I-85 on a desolate stretch, still running, driver's-side door wide open, headlights blazing, the contents of her purchases strewn along the highway shoulder, the contents of her purse spilled all over the front seat, her wallet and driver's license missing.

Baba drives the three of you to the Bhoumicks' house that evening, worry imprinting his face. Auntie and Uncle alternatively shout and weep at the audience gathered. Ma sits next to Auntie Bhoumick and holds her hand. You briefly venture to the basement, and find Krishna's makeshift photography studio, nothing out of place. The sound of footsteps overhead reminds you of thunder, an approaching storm. You unpin your favorite photograph of hers, the ocean and the shore, intending to take it. You turn over the picture and see her thin handwriting in pencil at the bottom right corner, *Gulfport 198—. Kyle.* You stand there for a long while, listening to the wind. You think you hear your mother call down to you, "Heera, are you there?"

"Coming," you reply, and hurriedly repin the photograph. You find the staircase, a headache starting to form behind your eyes. You reach the main floor and see that your mother has not left Auntie Bhoumick's side.

Baba steps out to speak with a group of men about organizing a search for the following day. In the dining room, the table is sparse except for a stainless steel pot of masala tea, a plastic tray of store-bought sugar cookies, foam cups and paper plates, cocktail napkins. From the window, you spy Krishna's little sister playing tag in the backyard with friends, chasing and being chased by other girls. Everyone in pigtails and tennis shoes. Anjuli stops when she spots you at the window, and waves.

As you get ready to leave, you see Ma speaking urgently with a pediatrician who lives in Cary and serves as a matchmaker in the community. As you walk up to them, Dr. Dey says, ". . . engagement all out of the question now, since this incident . . ."

Ma starts to say something but falls silent when you tug her sleeve. "Ma, we have to go."

Dr. Dey smiles at you.

Ma's glance at you projects weariness.

Baba appears out of nowhere, shakes Dr. Dey's hand, says, "We will call you tomorrow."

Road test

CRASH LEADS YOU BY THE HAND THROUGH THE DARK MAZE of parked cars, on the other side of the faux barn next to the farmers' pond and the sixteenth hole.

The country club took over years before and whitewashed everything—the barn, the fences, the cinder blocks that mark the start and end of the winding driveways, and the portico, where the Thompsons pull up in their red Cutlass, the color of fire ants, the color of the end of a cigarette on its last drag, the embers of a campfire. Crash's hand is dry while yours is clammy. Your teeth chatter a little and keep pleasant time with the way the heels of your shoes click-clack on the gravel.

You reach the Thompsons' car; the hood is still warm. You look Crash over, from neatly combed hair to uniformed shirt and khaki trousers, to shoes that shine even in the dark. He is the auto attendant, parking cars of the patrons tonight.

"What kind of revenge do you want?" you ask. "Nothing will ever be enough, so we should leave them alone." You want to tell him again that Marie would not like to be avenged this way. You want to tell him again that you are tired of being angry, that you are tired of being depressed, and that you want to leave Raleigh and go far away for college, that you want to leave and start over, that you want him to leave and start over too.

"They are the devils riding in this car," Crash says. "I want you to teach them a lesson."

You want to shake your head, but your head is blank. Is this what he's been thinking for the past year, planning revenge? "How?"

"You always have good ideas, Dia," he says. "Think of something."

You withdraw your hand, grateful he is leaving it up to you. "Let's climb the water tower again, Crash," you offer. "Make every drop turn the color of jaundice or the color of plague. Scare them silly when they turn on the tap or take a piss."

Crash laughs but his "No!" rings out like a bullet being discharged from a revolver.

A duel of silences follows. Your bodies are hardly five feet apart yet you are both alone, the sound of music from the cover band in the distance, a white woman trying to sing Donna Summer and the murmur of the mob of people drinking and eating, gossiping and no doubt getting high in the bathrooms in view of a woman in uniform, ready to hand out towels after the faucet narrows and the sink starts to empty.

You can tell that Crash wants another cigarette. He pats himself down while surveying rearview mirrors and empty backseats. He finds one. "What's the rush?" he asks, his voice unfurling with the smoke he exhales, and vanishing into the night. There is no moon out, yet the light from the country club makes every headlight twinkle and every car grill a cold smile.

You shiver despite the chorus of mosquitoes humming nearby, and bite the inside of your cheek.

"What's the rush?" he asks you again, but his voice is sharp now, as if he's lost you in the dark lot, as if he were left alone, speaking to himself.

You click your heels together and wish for calm. "I have an appointment tomorrow," you say, quietly, but your words linger and almost bounce between the cars that surround you both. "I need to go home and sleep."

Crash notices your tone. "You've got a date?" He laughs, incredulity in his voice.

You count in your head, to twenty. "An introduction."

Crash takes a long drag. "You're getting married? At nineteen?"

You shrug. "I still get to go to college," you say. "They promised me I could still go in New York." You keep talking, citing their promises like facts from a history book. Date, time, context.

"Dream on." Crash shakes his head. "They're just trying to get you to do what they want."

You can't help but agree, yet you question him. "Want?"

"So you don't end up like the girl on 85," Crash says. "You know her, right?"

Krishna. You want to nod but your silence is answer enough.

The Donna Summer song ends. "I just want to go." The promise of New York is a bright light, obscuring all details.

"So go." He presses the cigarette butt into the ground with the heel of his shoe. "But let me drive you home."

You hesitate. "If you leave now, you'll lose this job."

"You're worth it." He grins.

He drives slowly, as if you are the most precious cargo in the world, as if you will shatter if he brakes too hard or makes a sharp turn. You twist the knob on his car radio, but he shuts it off as soon as he hears an announcer's voice. You are a block away from home when he pulls over, gently parks in front an unlit house. He turns off the ignition, and sighs. "The Grimaldis are divorcing."

"Oh no," you say. "Oh no." You unbuckle your seat belt and reach for him.

He cries and cries, and the sleeve of your blouse is wet.

Hours later, Crash drives the last block and parks in front of your next-door neighbor's house. "I'll walk you in," he says, his hand at the small of your back. The air is humid and heavy, and somewhere not far away, a dog barks twice. You note how he sounds the time, this stranger dog: two barks for two o'clock.

"Nothing is going to happen to me if I go in alone," you say. "Luckily, prolonged scolding only annihilates the soul. My body will remain intact."

"I can explain," he says.

You shake your head. "The next time I use you as a reason to be out will come right after I renounce my family to become a Buddhist nun, and right before I shave my head and take a vow of silence."

Crash smiles. "So, you have a couple of weeks, then."

You laugh. "Definitely not tonight."

Bargaining

THE BRIDEGROOM'S PATERNAL UNCLE AND AUNT, THE Acharyas, arrive from their home outside Charlotte in their expensive Swedish car, deposit themselves at your front door. Their nephew is dressed as a candidate for office: khaki pants, blue button-down shirt, navy jacket. All that is missing is an oversized *Vote for Me* button. Neel smiles effortlessly and takes two samosas from the tray your mother offers.

Neel bears the gifts: a Tiffany vase for your mother, a Saks Fifth Avenue box for your father with a red silk tie inside; for you, a box wrapped in shiny pink paper and a satin pink bow atop. Inside a peacock-blue shawl, hand-stitched, no doubt, in India.

You thank him for the gift and he answers, "You're welcome," with a politician's bland ease.

Dr. Dey arrives late. The conversation is light and uncovers a distant connection. Your father's cousin's sister attended high school with Neel's mother, who is en route to New York from Kolkata as they speak. Dr. Dey's brother and Neel's father grew up on the same street, near Ballygunge.

Neel is handsome, wealthy. Twenty-six.

Ma and Baba are all pressed pleats and starched collars, all smiles. Ma makes luchi, channa daal, and lamb keema. She picks mint from the box of herbs growing by the patio for the chutney. Everyone compliments you on the cucumber raita you prepared.

You cannot remember a single moment of the mealtime chatter even as it is happening. You think of Marie as you look at the serving bowls, select her favorites. You manage to swallow two luchis with a dollop of raita. Ma produces a chocolate cake from a white bakery box when she serves cha in the living room, and you bite the inside of your cheek to keep from crying. After lunch Baba suggests you drive Neel up to the campus where Ma earned her library science degree.

Once you're in the car, you ask him to choose the music, and he finds the classical music channel. Mozart. Though you can't quite remember the name of the piece, you remember the first time you heard it: on a record player during rest time in kindergarten, Marie sitting next to you on the blue carpet slowly reading aloud *Curious George Makes Pancakes*. You now stifle both a yawn and the urgent desire to change the channel. You drive by one of the entrances to Kerr Lake, the green field and the clearing, the picnic tables and the boys who play Frisbee at the university, with long hair and beards, blond and brown-haired, white skin baking in the sun. So many girls as well, nice white girls who always seem to travel in pairs or trios, talking over one another and laughing.

You park the car and walk in the campus arboretum. He looks at the skyline in the distance as he asks you what you like to eat, what your favorite subjects are to study, what your favorite movie is.

You answers are polite and perfunctory.

He evades all of your questions about his life in New York, except to say that he enjoys the life he has with his family and friends.

He makes no move to touch you.

You drive home in silence. As you turn in to the entrance for the greater neighborhood, you see people walking their dogs on either side of the broad avenues. Most of the dogs are leashed and many of the leashes are taut. Your mother didn't like the unleashed dogs because they barked and chased after her sari or salwar kameez and double-knotted running shoes.

Recently you convinced her to wear yoga pants out when she walked. "Why should I have to change anything? Why can't they leash their dogs?" she asked, her arms crossed, her mouth set into the all too familiar stubborn line, and that was when you laughed. You remember saying: "That's what America is all about, Ma. Adapting to new situations. Doing things a new way."

Her mind was and then wasn't eight thousand miles away. Eventually she smiled and said almost absentmindedly, "But the street is not Burger King, it isn't do it your own way. They should follow the rules."

You laughed again. "This is America, Ma. Don't waste your life waiting for them to follow the rules."

You remember her shaking her head, but allowing you to pick out the yoga pants from the department store.

Now you glance at Neel and he is perfectly still, his head turned toward the window. You almost open your mouth to speak, but stop yourself, content to remain in your memory. One of the neighbors walking his dog waves as you drive by and you return the gesture.

Neel turns his head in time to catch your smile. He stares for a second and then closes his eyes.

Even as the afternoon is ending, Neel does not shake hands. Instead he puts both palms and fingertips together. Namaskar.

They leave and Ma and Baba look satisfied, as if the day were key lime pie, as if they'd consumed every crumb. "He's suitable," Ma says. Fatigue has left her easily tired, bony.

You stare at Baba. "Why doesn't he marry someone his own age?"

He says nothing, turns his gaze out the window.

"It's not uncommon in India for there to be such an age gap," Ma answers.

You want to feel something more than this disconnect: this distance and removal. You look at your mother's drawn face, the shadows forming under your baba's eyes, and you don't want to be too far from them. They have already turned down the son of an acquaintance because his family lives in Tallahassee and Baba says that's too far. You are left with more questions than answers.

"We're in North Carolina," you say. "Before this is set in stone, shouldn't we meet his parents? His dadu? Does he even have a dadu? A thakuma?" No one from that generation will react to this news; in their eyes, it is normal for the husband to be older, it is normal for the bride to be so young.

Ma tucks a strand of hair behind her ear. "My grandmother was married at nine, our mothers married at thirteen."

You gawk. "But Dadu let you wait. You got to go to college."

Ma shakes her head. "Well, my mother made him wait. She insisted that her only daughter have better than her fourth grade education. "

You turn toward Baba. "If Ma . . ."

Baba holds up his hand as if he were stopping oncoming traffic. "Our circumstances have changed." He looks at you. "The uncle who came today is the eldest in the family. Neel's grandparents are gone."

"So, it's the uncle's decision." Not a question as you intended.

Baba nods.

And you bite the inside of your cheek to keep yourself in

check, to keep from arguing about how patriarchy still makes the world go round.

Ma sighs, asks Baba to bring down some packing supplies from the guest room upstairs. She turns to ask you something but changes her mind, and grabs her car keys. After she pulls out a plastic bag from the trunk, your newish neighbor across the street, Mrs. Stone, comes out to her front porch. "Saw you had company," she says. "Friends or relatives?"

Her house looks like the *Partridge Family* house from the outside. You wonder why you always make these kinds of comparisons, and then you realize you don't know the insides of your neighbors' homes. People are friendly enough, once they learn your mother was educated at the nearby university, so that makes them academic siblings, fellow alums, once they realize the accents mean your parents speak other languages, that English is their second language or maybe even their third. On one occasion, Mrs. Stone questions Ma about her purple chiffon sari and matching purple bindi, and then Ma responds, her English modulated, that English is her third language after Bengali and Hindi.

Now you hear Ma's uncharacteristic laugh. "Hopefully a bit of both."

You turn away, feel heat rising from your belly to your cheeks.

You can be a stockbroker's wife. At nineteen. The promise of college in New York around the corner.

Or you could be a runaway.

Life as a road trip, Crash behind the wheel.

Everything uncertain.

You alive in your own skin and happy, answering to no one.

In your head you count the pickpocket proceeds under your mattress, and know it is not enough to disappear.

Krishna

YOU SEE HER FACE FLASH BEFORE YOU ON THE EVENING
news.

The TV announcer says that Alamance County officials have
not ruled out any possibilities, including homicide.

"We are continuing to investigate," says a tall man in a dark
suit to the reporter holding the microphone. "With each day that
passes, the chance that we will fully learn the truth of what happened a month ago diminishes."

A reward is now being offered.

The 800 number flashes across the bottom of the screen; then
a video begins of Krishna's parents and sister walking out of their
house and to their parked car. The little girl holds her parents'
hands. Her small face is serene, poised. You can't help but wonder
if Anjuli knows something the rest of her family does not.

Baba turns up the volume on the TV. He says something but
the announcer's voice drowns out everything else.

Ma gets up and turns off the set, and glares at him. "What
are you doing?"

Baba ignores her and looks over at you. "Do you know anything?"

You understand his frustration, his concern for his friends.
He has devoted many weekend mornings to combing the woods
and forests looking for her; all of the parents in their circle have

organized and expended hours and pushed back against their collective worry and fatigue to keep searching. All to no avail.

You shake your head.

Ma says, "I called them earlier today. It is a madhouse with the press — they've moved to a hotel for the next week."

You close your eyes but continue to see the images of Krishna's little sister holding on to each of her parents with her small hands, you see her hanging on to her life by inches. You think back to the roadmap of the United States you consulted in the library. New Orleans was less than a two-hour drive from Gulfport, the width of your index finger as you traced the route on the page.

You open your eyes in time to see your parents exchange glances and sigh.

Descent

WHY DO YOU ONLY NOTICE YOUR SURROUNDINGS WHEN you're leaving or entering? The clouds streak by your plane window as you head back to North Carolina. It's been more than a month since you received your diploma. You think about the things you can only begin to comprehend after a long absence. This much you know: in Raleigh, you long to escape. But in New York, you are away from Crash and your parents and you can go hours, even a full day, without thinking of them. Marie, you never forget. She resides in every heartbeat, in every step. You take her wherever you go: to the university, to the corner bagel shop in the mornings, on the subway as you try to find an art exhibit someone in your campus orientation group mentioned the day before. She is everywhere, and she hears your new acquaintances call you Dia.

Now as the flight attendants make their way down the aisles, you remember how Crash and Katrina sat together at graduation a few rows in front of you, whispering in each other's ears during the ceremony; how Katrina announced loudly she got into the honors program and that Crash was going too, to the private university in Durham; how Mr. and Mrs. Grimaldi sat apart in the family section, and congratulated you separately, though their sadness was identical; the moment of silence that followed the principal's announcement that Marie would receive an honorary degree and then the standing ovation.

You remember the way Crash hardly said congratulations or even goodbye. Once upon a time, you remember playing *The Waltons* game with him and Marie, back when you conspired to view the show together since it came on just before bedtime. You watched a particular episode and marveled at all of the siblings and their rivalries, and at the end of the program you'd mimic their good night rituals and then add your own.

"Good night, Anna Marie."

"Good night, Mary Ellen."

"Good night, Heera, my love."

"Good night, Elizabeth."

"Good night, John Boy."

"Good night, Jim-Bob Marco!" This became especially fun after Marie confessed that between Marco's first name and confirmation name, he was a real-life Jim-Bob, just like their dad.

Those days are long over.

You have been away at orientation and the summer program. Ma and Baba offered a graduation party but you turned them down, instead asking for this time away; and they agreed readily once they realized you'll be a married woman in the fall, and unable to live in undergraduate housing with people your own age. Their big plans for a capstone India trip postponed. Indefinitely.

You sit in a trance as the plane makes its slow descent, first the cloud mountains, and then the high blue of sky deepening as the pilot turns on the seat belt sign, tells you about the wind and the weather on the ground. You hear the wheels lower from their cubby in the underbelly of the plane and lock into place, your stomach drops as you approach your capital city. Raleigh is a city of trees and tiny forests. Raleigh is a city bifurcated by rivers and lakes. From the air Raleigh is green, and roads and buildings are threads and pieces from the Monopoly board game you haven't touched in years. For a long moment, you hold your breath and listen: the drone of the engines, the flight attendant's bored voice. You glance away from the window for a second and see everyone around you sitting back in their chairs; some close their eyes, a woman in a tweed jacket takes off her glasses and rubs the bridge of her nose where the spectacles rested. You turn back to the portal window and now you have a better view: the buildings in the distance look taller, and the trees become distinct sentient beings. The gold from the sun turns the river silver and the roads and neighborhoods look like a jigsaw puzzle, or a series of terrible scars after an accident.

You are so low that you can see the shadow of the airplane already touching down.

The plane lands and comes to a long stop. As it taxis off the runway, you sigh.

You are home again, Raleigh, your wedding looming on the horizon.

Second hand

YOU KNOW YOU MIGHT SEE CRASH, BEFORE THE CEREMONY, in the long hallway, lingering under the recess lights, leaving his station where the knives are sharpened and the stainless steel bowls reflect like mirrors, risking this latest job to catch a glimpse of you as you enter from the front foyer, a live picture bride resplendent in red and gold. So you stand very still as the aunties, the women in your parents' spidery social web minus Krishna's mother, who has gone to India, hover over you with more face powder, a deeper blush, and safety pins to keep the pleats of your silk sari in place.

The aunties ask, a hint of metal underneath their whisper-soft voices, "Do you want more bangles for this arm, Heera?"

Your eyes hurt when you look at them. "Yes," you say.

The aunties ask, "Can we paint your face more?"

"Yes," you say, closing your eyes.

The aunties ask, "Can we affix the veil?"

"Yes," you say.

They drape it over you but the plaits of your hair do not cooperate with the red gauze threaded with gold. Anita Auntie bobby pins your plaits, her hands smoothing the braid, and you are back at the beginning of high school, the last time you rode the bus, the afternoon some boys sitting behind you put their chewed gum in your hair. Marie instructed you in pig Latin not to cry, cursed at the older boys in a low voice, and Marco leaned in to the driver as you got off the bus and complained that they were exposing themselves. Ma couldn't get out the myriad of tiny pieces so she prepared to cut at the nape. Marie held your hand as you wept then, while Marco told Ma to wait. He ran all the way to his house, grabbed the jar of Skippy out of his mother's cabinet, and ran back. "Try this," he said. "I read that it works." Ma and Marie slathered peanut butter over the gum knots; Marco entertained you with card tricks until your hair dried. And the Hubba Bubba pieces slid off in the sink when Ma washed your hair. Success.

You know Crash's mother will be in the audience, a satisfied look on her face, congratulating herself that her son hasn't married the one girl she finds unacceptable. The one girl who was her dead daughter's best friend. The one girl who was with her daughter when she was fatally injured. But you also know Crash is not on good terms with his mother and father, and cannot enter the hotel as their guest. You know his only ticket to the wedding is through the double swinging doors that lead from the kitchen to the beige hallway and on to the conference room that your parents have chosen in lieu of the grand ballroom. To save money. Your parents booked the Hindu temple in Morrisville, but because of the vandalism after the Klan march last month, it is not quite finished. So this hotel in downtown Raleigh moved from second to first choice.

You find yourself alone for a moment, after the aunties successfully drape the veil, then pack up their bottles and brushes and stow them away in their rolling suitcases for another day and another Bengali bride.

You open your eyes.

The dressing room has a wall composed entirely of mirrors and you see yourself in the distance, as if you are looking at a mannequin through a department store window. The borrowed gold weighs around your neck. Your parents are renting everything but the bride. You hold your breath, hear the second hand tick on the wall clock above the door frame, and begin calculating the number of steps you will need to take to leave the hotel, hail a taxi, and run away.

But then the door opens behind you and your mother enters, holding something minute on the tip of her finger.

You exhale. It is the sound of the wind combing through the trees, it is almost a whistle.

Your mother walks around and you see her through the mirror. She reaches up to your forehead and you feel something sticking in place just between the eyes.

"Go see, Heera," your mother says. "Promila Auntie brought it back from India. It matches."

A gold-flecked bindi.

A third eye.

Sightless.

Your own painted face is unrecognizable in the wall of mirrors, and the smile your mother wears is just as unrecognizable, especially with all of the heavy makeup covering her perpetual fatigue. You turn around and look past your mother to the windows and envy the tree branches and the leaves, how they soak up the sun and stay warm. You shiver as your thoughts inevitably return to Crash.

You know you shouldn't ask.

You know Ma isn't going to tolerate your disobedience now, just as the wedding is to commence. You are alone for the first time in days, your mother smiling for the first time in nearly a month. You hear the crowd coming in, and people talking and milling about. Someone's young son or daughter plays a few measures of "Blue Moon" on the grand piano that is in the foyer under the oversized chandelier, and then the music stops abruptly. You picture Crash as the bridegroom, for just a moment, a silk kurta shirt covering the tattoos on his chest, before you remember him at eighteen, the last night of the water tower in Apex, a rope tied around his waist and a paintbrush in his hand, as he swung back and forth and painted the anarchy symbol in red, big enough for people miles away to see. A scarlet letter to brand the town the water tower serviced. Whatever the *A* stood for in the Hawthorne novel or in society, in your life it ended up representing one word. *Absence.*

"I think he's in the kitchen working today," you say. "Can I go see him?"

The last time you asked your mother for permission to visit Crash was just after Marie's funeral, he curly-haired, unshaven, and blind with grief. The images you recall every time you have thought of him after Marie's death are distorted, like a sooty film over the skin.

Incredulity gallops across Ma's face, and it is the same look as when you first arrived to prepare for the wedding, when you stepped through the front door, suitcase in your hand. You'd been away at the university, in New York; maybe she didn't believe you'd return once the monthlong summer program was completed. Still the tuition for the coming year had not been paid, but Baba said he was working on a plan.

Crash had been at the airport baggage claim, leaning up against a pillar, waiting for you to walk through the terminal and fetch your belongings. He'd lit a cigarette, one hand cupped over the instant flame of the lighter. His stance and leather jacket re-

minded you of a raw James Dean. Somehow he had known you
were coming home that day. You also knew your father would be
circling the airport, unwilling to pay for parking, listening to the
understated tones of the announcer on public radio. So you had
been alone when you saw Crash by the baggage carousel, a package in his hand.

"How are you here?" you'd asked, standing before him, your
heart filling the cavernous room like the smoke coming out of his
mouth. You swallowed all of the snide remarks that were bubbling
in your throat, about Katrina.

He showed up, after all.

Alone.

Crash dropped his cigarette, smashed it with the heel of his
shoe, and gently blew smoke away from your face. "I had to be the
first to welcome you home, Dia," he said as he hugged you. His
kiss was chaste and dry on your cheek. He handed you the package, wrapped in plain brown paper, then pulled your bag off the
rolling belt and laid it at your feet.

You tried to return the parcel but he said it was for you. Something to open later.

You unzipped your backpack and carefully put it away.

"Look me up sometime," he said. "I'm in the usual places." He
laughed a little.

"Let's have a drink now," you'd suggested.

He smiled. "Your old man has circled the terminal six times—
you need to go. Just come see me, before you go through with this."

You wanted to open the package the first night you were home,
right after your parents had cleared the dinner dishes. You knew
you had the courage at that moment, the curiosity. But you heard
your father walk heavily up the staircase calling your name, and

you buried the present in your closet with some papers from high school you wanted to keep.

You tried so hard to open the package, the next day, the day after that. Every day, as your mother kept you busy with preparations, as your father kept watch over you ("Capital of Mozambique? Capital of New Zealand?") even as you trotted to the end of the driveway to fetch the *News & Observer* or check the mailbox.

But the courage inside you ebbed and you set it aside.

Earlier today, on the morning of your wedding, you woke before dawn and took the package out from your closet. The house was quiet and dark and the world on the other side of your bedroom window matched. You turned on your study light and sat on the carpet, ripped the brown paper off and found last year's yearbook underneath, the familiar Spartans helmet in crimson and navy blue. The Grimaldis had paid extra, and there underneath the year was Marie's name etched in block letters. You blinked back tears as you cracked open the spine. On the second page, Crash had written you a note and paper clipped it to the table of the contents: *D—She would have wanted you to have this. Look on p. 60—C.*

You wanted so much to take the day and pore over every page, but you knew you couldn't, and your breathing became labored and slow. You ran across the sports teams, and stopped on swim & dive, Katrina's eyes piercing you from the page along with April Stewart's, and one of the Kaminski brothers; Mr. Cleveland with his arms crossed, in a jacket marked COACH. You thought back to the tryouts years before, how Marie and Marco declined Mr. Cleveland's invitation to join because your parents wouldn't let you compete. "All for one and one for all," Marco had said.

You heard Baba's alarm on the nightstand and you exhaled. You turned to the page Crash wanted you to see, and there, in black and white, was a candid shot of you and Marie at the carnival, Dorothy and the Scarecrow, arm in arm, mouths open in song.

Finally your mother answers. "Now, before you see your new husband and marry him in front of all of my friends, you want to enter the hotel kitchen in your wedding dress to meet a dishwasher, Heera?"

You wonder how she knows Crash works as a dishwasher.

You could stay silent, you should, what with all of your bangles sparkling on your arms, earrings from your grandfather weighing down your lobes—the red silk sari heavy on your body, a tiny tiara to keep the wedding veil in place. You could remain a doll—after you marry you won't have the luxury of visiting your friends, even the estranged ones, the ones you couldn't live without, the one who once saved your life. But your mother doesn't really know.

What Ma knows about Marco's family is the mathematics of what everyone in town thought they knew, how Marco's father left, how Marco's mother seemed to carry through the years of Marco's antics and Marie's death with the aplomb of a woman watching Sunday theater from the balcony, binoculars in one hand and a glass of cognac in another; how she worked after Marie's death, and went into town and bought a rack of black pantsuits, mannish blouses with big collars, and lipstick, how she spent every Tuesday at the salon, and then every other day of the week selling houses, one or two at a time, to strangers who wanted to buy into the charm of their small corner of the Raleigh community, wide lawns, smoke from the backyard barbeques, and little girls on pink bicycles pedaling into the woods. You know Ma gossiped with the aunties at the Indian dinner parties on the weekends—but all the talk flying through the air wasn't going to bring Marie back from the dead.

You say, "My name is Dia."

Ma's lips compress into a flat line.

You say, "I have to say goodbye to him." Your voice firm and clear, unlike your appearance as a picture bride, who is admired but does not speak.

"You have had years to say goodbye, Heera," Ma says, her eyes averted from the window and the mirrored wall. "You have had the last month since you came home."

"I wasn't ready," you say.

Ma opens her mouth to speak but closes it and swallows a few times; and opens it again.

The music of the ceremony begins, the mournful shehnai, and the crowd's din diminishes and then is silenced as if the guests have left and the room stands empty.

"It's too late," Ma says.

Moonless night

NEEL STOPS SMILING THE MINUTE THE DOOR CLOSES AND the last of the well-wishers joke about visiting the maternity ward nine months from tonight.

You look at each other. The bride doll and the groom doll still and silent. You wonder if you can plead a headache on your wedding night.

He seems to read your mind: "I'm tired," he says, and walks into the bathroom, locking the door behind him.

You stand there for a long moment, then slowly start to take off your wedding jewelry.

You look around the hotel room, and your mind goes blank. The honeymoon has been postponed until Christmas, when just the four of you, all four Acharyas, will do a whirlwind tour of India. You are slated to fly back to New York tomorrow after the post-wedding brunch, you are taking up residence with your in-laws in New York City. Your parents will move to Jackson Heights at the end of the month, close but not next door, close to the clinic where Ma will be treated.

New family

THEY ARE THE KIND OF FAMILY WHO DON'T EAT MACHER jhol with their hands. They prefer a knife and fork for every meal, even snacks like samosa chaat. They are the kind of family who insist on traveling first class on airplanes, who stay in hotels in India, opting out of the cramped sleeping arrangements and late night adda with their closest relatives. They insist on proper attire, even to go to the corner store for milk. They have no issues spending hundreds of dollars on a pair of shoes as well as raising money for a Kali mandir planned near Baldwin Station, as long as their names are listed as founding donors. They have tons of acquaintances, and you cannot keep track of anyone. It's not like North Carolina where, despite political factions, there is still one Durga Puja in October and one Saraswati Puja in January. Here there are eight pujas in the greater New York area, and because of politics, you find yourself hopping from one venue to another. You spend more time in a taxi than you do reciting the Gayatri mantra in front of the lavishly adorned goddess, her face smiling, tranquil for eternity.

Neel's father is kind to you, but formal. He wears silver-rimmed glasses that match the silver of his hair. He is the first to ask after the health of your parents at the end of the day.

Neel's mother is thin as paper and sports a wavy bob. She praises your beauty to anyone and everyone she encounters, the

shopgirls, the mail carrier, and the doorman, as if you're not standing next to her when she speaks.

Neel is polite. Neel calls his parents "Mom" and "Dad" and
insists you do the same. Neel smiles at his father's jokes. Neel
praises his mother's cooking, that is when his mother cooks; that
is, when he's home to eat and not out with his friends. Neel's mom
is an expert hostess and keeps the name of her Indian caterer a secret from all the aunties who come to the apartment on weekends.
Neel sleeps in the same bed as you, with his back turned.

The theory of the arrangement is that you can visit your parents as much as you like. But in practice, you hardly see your parents except for puja and major functions where both sets of parents
are invited. You can see Ma and Baba, but come dinnertime, you
must be back at the apartment. There is never an opportunity to
spend the night. Your visits with them are often rushed, between
Ma's visits to the clinic and Baba's increasingly infrequent con-
sulting work that takes him out of their apartment. While Neel
talks a good game on the phone and promises to visit, he does not
accompany you. Your in-laws are very observant but do not correct
their son in front of you.

One day you test the boundaries of this agreement, visiting
your parents at the end of a busy day at the university. Ma and
Baba are surprised, but pleased.

"I'll make daal," Ma says.

"I'll make cha," Baba says.

After dinner, you read poetry aloud from your English class textbook, some Emily Dickinson, some Langston Hughes. When
you sit down to write a brief response paper, nothing sticks. Your
parents watch you rip out the notebook paper from your binder,
crumple it up, and throw it away. They talk about fate and kapal,

and you know no one really believes that. You go into the kitchen and turn on the radio, the little transistor that used to accompany you on the occasional trips to the beach. You talk about your philosophy professor's definitions of free will.

Later, when the Rush song comes on the radio, you explain the lyrics to Baba.

"I have no idea what they're saying," Ma says afterward. "It goes too fast."

All of you laugh. The first real laughter since you've moved to New York.

Baba glances at his watch. "It's late, sona."

"She can stay over one night," Ma counters.

"I'll call them later," you say, unwilling to break this spell of newly found peace.

Baba nods, and rises to make more cha.

You talk about the students in your classes, how they're different from your classmates in North Carolina. Most are like you, not longtime residents of New York.

Ma retells the story of going to North Carolina with a new baby in her arms. You haven't heard this one in a long time. "After New York, I thought I'd landed on the back side of Mars. I think I asked your baba six times that first week if the airlines had made a mistake, if they had transported us outside of the United States to some distant land."

Baba sat down, steam rising from his cup, adding how unwelcomed they were at first, how their neighbors and townspeople were careful, aloof to the point of madness. Everything closed— the grocery, the dry cleaner, the hardware store—when the banks did. No late night trips to the store, a marked change from the twenty-four-hour bustle of New York. Luckily, Merrick's Convenience opened up around the same time as the 7-Eleven.

"We lived on snacks for a long while," Ma said, laughing.

You want to ask about Mr. Grimaldi, about when Marco and Marie were born, but the telephone rings.

Baba answers. His salutation is pleasant enough, but he pales slightly. "Of course, of course," he says, his Bengali smooth. "Yes, she'll be ready." He hangs up and looks at Ma instead of you. "Mr. Acharya will arrive in thirty minutes."

You and Ma sigh in unison.

You wonder which one, you wonder if your husband is finally keeping his word. You ask, "Neel?"

Ma leaves the table, and you hear her water cup clatter in the sink a moment later.

"Abhik-Da," Baba answers. Your father-in-law.

"Why can't I stay?"

Baba says, "You're a married woman now."

One evening, Neel comes into the apartment, shoulders drooping. You and Mom and Dad are watching the news, one year after the fall of the Berlin Wall, half a million people lining the streets. He waves off everyone's questions, and asks you to go shopping with him.

His parents beam from the love seat.

You say yes.

You leave the apartment, and on the street you shudder, hit by a sudden gust of wind that has barked down the street and is already onto the next corner.

"It's Mom's birthday," he says, taking you by the elbow.

"What?" you ask. "Today?"

He shakes his head. "Soon." He smiles. "I thought it would be nice if we got her something together."

He hails a cab, and you are whisked off to a jewelry store.

There you pick out a bejeweled pendant, a rose sparkling with red stones. "It's different," you say. "I have never seen anything like it."

He nods and reaches for his wallet. "Thank you."

After you leave the store, you walk for a while until you reach a department store. It has closed for the evening, but still he peers in. "I can't see my own reflection in the window," he says.

"You're standing too close, that's why." You look at the window from where you stand, behind him. At once, you see the fine tweeds and silks that are displayed in bolts, it seems, right through the reflection of the awnings of the travel agency and the Thai restaurants across the street. It is transparent. There are little streaks of gray sky at the top of the window. And the gray ink spot that is your husband. Your eyes turn toward the mannequins in the next window. Tall and all brunette heads thrown back carelessly, hair tossed in defiance and flirtation. Such nice clothes. What really captures your attention are the umbrellas. You have lost yours on the subway, and it is beginning to rain. The umbrellas look like sunspots, bright and yellow and spiral-patterned. Little red dots hang before your eyes, again. You blink them away, with a silent prayer.

Neel steps back from the window and turns around to face you. "Let's start over," he says, sticking out his hand as if to shake yours. "I'm Neel, your husband. Sorry I've been such an ass."

You laugh and take his hand.

Silhouettes

THE SUN HAS SET AND THE MACKEREL CLOUDS DISSIPATE. You sit on the biggest log, away from Neel and his friends. They are gathered by the bonfire, they laugh and drink and re-tell stories. They do not remember you and you do not want to remember them, or this moment. You will never be one of them, they are older with degrees and occupations and futures, and they are untethered in their independence. They have stories and his-tories that predate you, and it is clear from their faces that the title of Neel's wife was not supposed to go to you. Many of them say hello but some call you Rita instead of Heera, then quickly drift away to friends. Neel is sometimes kind when it's the two of you, but in gatherings among his friends, he looks at you as though you're a stranger and does not speak to you except on the ride home. "Wasn't that great?" he asks before he turns on the radio and drowns out your reply.

Neel is like modern plumbing, he runs hot and cold. There are weeks, months even, where he remembers your name and offers to take you to a movie and out for a drink after work. But his prev-alent mood is the dark sky just before a downpour; he leaves the apartment before breakfast and returns just as you finish dinner.

Someone turns on the transistor and it is the second half of "Should I Stay or Should I Go?" They are dancing silhouettes against the orange flames. You wonder if your whole life will be like this, wondering and wishing aloud for things that are so far away you may as well be wishing for one of Saturn's rings, one of Jupiter's moons. The stars are impossibly plentiful tonight, not an inch of sky is wasted. You look until you see the Big Dipper. You remember Marco's presentation, the way he could spin a myth about the stars. You wonder if you can walk away, but you are so unprepared. Maybe you can walk away a week from now, a month from now, when you're ready.

You wake to the unmistakable sound: Neel laughing. The sun is still asleep, your husband's side of the bed is empty. Your eyes are too bleary, you cannot make out the numbers on the clock. At first you think he's speaking to his father or mother. He does not sleep well, you have often found him speaking to his father during the darkest part of the night during the past nine months when everyone should be asleep. You usually spy on them in the living room or sharing a sandwich at the kitchen table. They usually sense your presence and stop speaking and wait for you to return to the bedroom.

Tonight, you tiptoe down the hall and see the door firmly shut to your in-laws' bedroom, the lights off in the kitchen.

You come to stand outside the room he infrequently uses as a study.

The door is closed.

And yet his laughter echoes.

There is a small TV in that room but you don't hear anything but Neel's voice and the squeak of the executive chair's wheels as he leans back in the seat.

"Gotta go now," he says. "I love hearing your voice . . ."

And then a promise to visit. Soon.

And then a declaration of love. Forever.

You grit your teeth, tiptoe back to the bedroom.

Lunchtime blues

MA LIKENS THE CHOICE TO GOING TO THE SARI SHOP. "EVeryone looks through the window before they even step in through the doorway, and they see a beautiful gold-studded sari on a naked mannequin, and they say, 'That one. I want that gaudy thing.'" She sips her cooled tea, nibbles on the caramel-coated wafer on the edge of the porcelain saucer. The restaurant busy, but the lunch crowd thins out to a few tables. Yours the only one at the bay window, still occupied.

You look out at the clouds spread over the horizon, like a repeating pattern of wallpaper. "Mannequins cannot be naked, Ma," you say, surprised at how cross you sound. "Only unclothed."

Ma's sipping and nibbling don't abate. She pauses to smile and then continues. "I went into that store, and I was able to get the best item for the best price," she says. "And to this day you have never thanked me for that."

Your mouth hangs open for a moment. "You weren't clothes shopping, Ma." You clench your teeth to keep from saying anything more.

"Anyway, once you wear that same sari for a little while, you want to change clothes. Find something new." Ma laughs. "In our family, we are taught not to want too many new things."

You take the remainder of the cookie off Ma's saucer, and pop it into your mouth. When you finish chewing, you say, "Well, as you are fond of pointing out, I didn't grow up there."

You cannot help but count the months since your marriage commenced.

Has it been almost a year and a half?

You are rudderless. Your parents cannot borrow more and can no longer afford your college tuition. The scholarship is not enough. It is said that money cannot buy happiness, but you know that's not true. The tuition indeed bought you a few hours each day where you were among your peers, talking poetry and philosophy, complaining about homework and papers and tests, attending seminars, planning semester by semester for the future. You hadn't quite settled on a major but you had already planned to enroll in a photojournalism class for the following term.

Your in-laws do not offer to pay; they say it is your parents' responsibility. "We'll see," your father-in-law says, and it sounds suspiciously like a no.

Your mother-in-law makes pointed jokes about being a grandmother. "Perhaps you'll find the means to complete your education once my grandsons arrive," she says.

You have been forced to withdraw.

Neel is running cold again, he barely lives at the apartment. He doesn't come home until his parents retire for the evening; he barely speaks to you but still manages to crawl into your shared bed more often than not.

You stare at Ma until the waiter returns with the check. Her face is haggard under the heavy makeup but her eyes are strong and clear. She has been going to the clinic regularly for treatment. Baba found them an apartment not too far from the famed Patel Brothers grocery, not too far from the clinic. The waiter first tries to hand it to you. You drop your gaze to see the amount on the bill, and then look up at the mustached man in the oversized shirt. "I'll pay for it."

Ma laughs, opens her purse and tosses her credit card toward the waiter. "No, that's all right. I'll get it."

You smile sweetly. "Thank you for the free meal."

The waiter smiles, bewildered, and then walks away.

"It would be different if you had a baby."

You hide your disappointment by digging your nails into your palm. "I tell you that I think Neel is dating someone and that's your solution?"

Ma shrugs.

You look out the window again. A delivery man parks his car in a loading zone, grabs a thermal box, and rushes through the door of the building across the street.

"I wouldn't be watching the meter maid right now," Ma says.

You mumble, point out to Ma how the parking police is inching down the street.

"Keep trying," Ma says. "Persistence will lead to great rewards."

How do you tell your mother that your husband is simply not interested? In a way that she can understand?

You turn your eyes back to the door, willing the delivery boy to come out, jump in his car and drive away, beat the odds, avoid the ticket. You place your hands from the edge of the table into your lap. How cold they have become, two blocks of ice, numb and unable to feel anything.

"Don't ignore me, Heera," Ma says. The waiter returns with the credit card charge slip. She signs, dismisses the young man with a nod.

"Dia," you say.

She turns her head.

"I'm not a defective machine," you find yourself countering, your voice barely above a whisper. "You can't just replace some parts and expect better results."

The meter maid comes upon the delivery car and bestows a pink ticket onto the glass. The deliveryman comes outside. You judge him to be roughly your age. Unshaven, disheveled, but handsome in an undergraduate student kind of way. He smiles at the meter maid, and says something. The woman changes out the pink slip for a warning yellow.

You stand up. "I have to use the bathroom," you say to your mother.

"I'll go with you," Ma says, placing the napkin that was on her lap into the empty soup bowl in front of her.

"As you wish."

The ladies room only has one toilet. You let Ma go ahead. As soon as she closes the door behind her, you slip out the front of the restaurant. The deliveryman long gone but the meter maid still delivering bad news to a row of parked cars.

You clear your throat. "Excuse me," you say to the woman you startled by touching her on the shoulder. "What did he say to you?"

"Mercy," she says, flashing her green eyes.

Blessings

YOU ARE STRANDED AT YOUR BACHELOR UNCLE-IN-LAW'S place, not even two miles from your in-laws' apartment. Although the traffic outside was tightly packed, the traffic inside the paper-thin walls and on the shabby chic couches is reminiscent of the mob watching the games in the Colosseum. Uncles and aunties everywhere, everyone speaking at once, and questioning you: "Why aren't you eating this? Why don't you have a baby yet? Did you see where I put my purse? Where is your husband? Where is your husband? Where is your husband?"

You look around the room, the smell of aftershave and rose water mingling, so much sweat underneath the folds of the saris and the tight bodices that cover the breasts and leave the midriffs exposed. A commingling of smells as well, the curried lentils and rice, turmeric that has been overcooked and has stuck to the bottom of the pan, the fried smell from the tray of samosas that are starting to grow cold, the divergence between the masala chai and the pungent black coffee, on two competing tables, spigots off and on, on and off.

Everyone waiting for the priest to start the puja, another January, another ceremony to bless the new year and the books, the instruments the students have dragged through the snow to this apartment crowded with bodies and sitars and guitars and flutes, men and women whose shoes were left scattered in the hallway that leads to the outdoor world.

*

You look around and still can find neither your husband nor your mother. Your father-in-law, a distinguished version of your husband, catches your eye and mouths the words, *Sit down. We're about to start.* He joins the priest on tiny handmade rugs in front of the goddess adorned in a yellow sari, her many limbs bearing shiny ornaments.

So you take your place among the aunties on the carpeted floor, a bedsheet with a pattern of garish peacocks in every square. There isn't much room. Some auntie's elbows nudge you in the ribs. Another auntie complains loudly, trying to get her voice above the din, trying to make herself heard over the crowd that has not quieted, that sounds like a gaggle of geese, and what with the traffic outside those dirty windows, a busy Saturday in winter, not even the snow and ice and high winds could keep these men and women and children from clustering around the goddess, her fine features etched in balsa wood.

Finally that second auntie says, "My god it is hot."

It is hot. You keep your head down and stare at the peacock pattern, the flourish of the feathers, and the pattern of eyes that cannot see. Someone rings the bell twice, someone else walks hurriedly to the door before the bell chimes for a third time. Your father's voice echoes as he opens the door. You cannot see him from where you sit but imagine the surprise on his face as he greets his own wife and son-in-law. "How did you come to be outside?" he asks. "I've been looking everywhere for you."

Your mother's laugh brittle.

Your husband's loud exclamation: "We were searching for you."

You hear the catch in his voice, and know he is lying, and your mother laughs again and you know there is more to their story than being locked out of the apartment, alone in the hallway with each other and forty pairs of shoes underfoot.

Then your father gasps. "Oh, you."

A hush replaces the din as your father-in-law and the priest begin intoning the Sanskrit prayers. You look up from the un-blinking gaze of the parrots as your husband and parents enter the room and sit on the edge of the sheet, side by side. A figure stand-ing behind them, a man at once familiar, but unfamiliar among the aunties and uncles.

Crash enters, wearing a kurta and slacks, and striped socks, sporting a healthy and well-rested visage, and smelling like fresh snow. The priest concludes the first set of prayers and everyone watches him throw flowers to the ground, at the feet of the god-dess. You cannot sit still through the priest's intonations, the can-delabra that is rolled up cotton balls doused in ghee, the aunties who reek, all jostling for more legroom as they crowd the hallway, angling for a better view.

You cannot remember the words to the song that has just be-gun on the harmonium. Ma glares at you, three bodies deep, across the carpet covered with sheets, and mouths the words, *Just try.* You cannot, Crash is too close. Your body now rigid, cheeks alternating hot and cold, blush to frost to blush again. You cannot bear his equanimity, the ironed clothes on his back, washed hair, smell of his soap wafting by you. He gazes not at you but the serene face of the goddess, the perfect cheekbones, kohl-smudged eyes. You only relent and exhale after you notice his hands, unadorned and balled into fists, knuckles white, skin taut.

You smile, clear your throat, begin to sing.

༄

You and Crash start at opposite ends of the long banquet table, easily forty people between you, not employing the provided utensils, but instead utilizing their fingers to pick up the sweetmeats, and cubed pears and apples. They use their own plastic spoons for moa, the gluey rice balls soaked in molasses turning your fingertips sticky; and the cream-colored yogurt cooked at home in an earthen pan and sweetened with condensed milk. You do not care for any of the sweets, pick all of Crash's favorites from when he was a child and still came to your house: the laddoo made with chickpea flower and dyed the color of sunflowers, chom-chom soaked in rose water and spongy in ultra sweet syrup, dates and cherries in concentric bowls at the center of the table. You take none of the things you like, the spiced nuts, the rice flour snacks dusted with chili powder and tossed like a salad with chopped cucumber and mint chutney. Eventually you and Crash meet in the middle of the line. He smiles and trades his plate, heaped with samosas and coriander chutney, for yours.

"So you live here now?" you ask.

"If you mean New York, then yes," he replies.

"What about school?"

"Finished early," he says. "What about you?"

"Taking a break," you say, not wanting to blurt out the truth here in front of your family and their friends.

Like a dutiful wife, you take the plate of snacks to your husband, standing six places back in the line, talking in a hushed tone to a cousin, a frown on his upper lip and above his eyebrows. The pulse in his temple looks like a knot in a plank of wood, and you regret that you ever married him, that you ever did anything to see him so ugly in his unhappiness. You look at him, and say, "Take this."

"It's the last one," Crash says, his voice booming behind you. "Who knows when the next batch will come out of the oven?"

Neel takes the plate and the cousin takes Crash's, without thanks, and they resume their conversation. Crash takes you by the elbow into the kitchen, where caterers expertly pour lassi into Dixie cups and garnish each serving with a sprig of mint. The man closest to the swinging double doors says, "We are not ready yet."

"No worries," Crash says, "just passing through." He takes you to the other side of the kitchen and pushes you through a doorway, into an alcove that miraculously holds a door that leads into a guest room, a queen-sized bed with an impersonal royal blue bedspread covering it, a table with a couple of books with Bengali titles on them, a stainless steel tray with party favors.

"You know this apartment well," you remark. You look closer at the tray and find the party favors to be tiny books containing the serenity prayer.

"Slept here before," he says. "Usually alone."

"What?"

"He's my sponsor," Crash says.

"What are you thinking, bringing me in here? This is the bedroom of my uncle-by-marriage."

"I wanted to be the one to tell you," Crash says.

"What?"

He smiles. "Katrina said yes."

You break free of his tethering arm and flee.

Found & lost

YOU RUN INTO CRASH SEVERAL MONTHS LATER OUTSIDE A market in Elmhurst. "You're here now?"

He nods. Stubble on his cheeks, his eyes are bloodshot. "Come over. I'm just down the street."

You don't have to be home for a couple of hours. You agree.

You enter the lobby and he greets the doorman, who tells him the elevator is out again. You walk up three flights of stairs, groceries in tow. "Can I put the milk in your fridge?" you ask.

"If you can find room," he answers. The apartment is tiny, and definitely all Crash. He has stacked his considerable cassette collection against the wall that separates the bedroom from the bathroom, a small rectangle painted a sick green with a wan fluorescent bar twitching and shaking. Crash keeps the light on but closes the door after you peek in. Looking at the space between the bottom of the door and the floor, it appears as though the bathroom is occupied, someone is moving around in there. From the windowsill on the other side of the room, the wall of plastic tape covers look as though invading armies of ants have attacked it, tiny black scrawls of handwriting on white paper covering every space. But every word is legible to him. Crash knows exactly what music is in those cassettes, and knows the order: it is obvious only to him, this non-alphabetical non-chronological arrangement from floor to ceiling, from east to west on an entire wall.

But you know Crash's order as well as you know your own face. It is the music of the city, the thumping, loud music of the city that you and Crash loved but were never allowed to listen to when you were growing up. The Clash, the Smiths, Depeche Mode, Run DMC, Salt-N-Pepa; the musicians and artists who rebelled against the system with asymmetrical hair, safety pins as jewelry, clothes that exhibited their defiant spirit.

"You're going to live here after your wedding?"

Crash grins. "Katrina thinks this place is a dump." He shrugs. "It's mine." It's rent-controlled. He tells you he has to move to the nice place Katrina has found for them after the wedding, close to the college where she's getting her MBA, but he is going to keep this place as an art studio, a place to pursue his photography when he's not working for his future father-in-law at the World Trade Center.

"What do you want to listen to?"

"Play 'How Soon Is Now?'" you suggest.

But Crash doesn't listen, he goes straight to the heart of the middle column of cassettes, and plugs his choice with an emphatic click. Soon Bono croons, "I Still Haven't Found What I'm Looking For" and you sigh. Music that Marie listened to, loved. He plays the entirety of *Joshua Tree* before he switches to the radio. He doesn't reply to any of your questions, and you don't tell him where you live with your husband and his parents—but sense he knows much more about you than he lets on. "Are you going to stay the night here?"

He nods but doesn't say anything.

He heats up sake in a double boiler on the tiny stove, washes out a special glass.

"What about your sponsor?" you ask.

His eyes are glassy. "What are you talking about?"

You think of your uncle-in-law's apartment and the puja and decide you must have misunderstood. You pace around the apartment, itch to clean it but stop yourself.

He drinks everything he has heated in the pan.

You come out of the bathroom to see him passed out as the sun sets over the buildings across the Hudson River.

You leave him a note before hauling your groceries back down the stairs: *I'll be back tomorrow.*

But you don't go back for a while, not until the next time Neel doesn't come home after work, and his father offers a bland excuse about seeing old friends, his mother offers to make popcorn and watch a movie with you. "I think they're showing *The Prince of Tides* on TV," she says.

You smile at them, grab your backpack and camera, and tell them you're off to take photos of the coming sunset.

You walk briskly all the way, intoning Marie's first, middle, and last names like a prayer. Anna Marie Grimaldi.

You think of everything you want to say, a litany of grievances. You are going to tell him about the university, about your in-laws. You are going to tell him that you want to disappear.

You show up at Crash's building and the doorman recognizes you.

You knock a few times.

You hear voices.

Crash finally comes to the door, shirtless, hair wild, reeking of sweat and a cheap perfume Katrina would never buy in a million years. "Dia!"

You burst in expecting to find someone else, but it is strangely empty except for the two of you. Your desire to scream outweighs your desire to push him to the ground. "What are you doing?"

He doesn't answer. He turns away. You can tell he's looking for a shirt.

You have so many questions to ask, you have so much to say, and this will turn out to be another missed moment. He looks dazed with sex. "What are you thinking? Are you thinking? You can find your brain north of your neck."

He turns back around, smiles slowly, looks you over, forehead to sneakers. His eyes finally rest on your face. "You came here on a Friday night to check on me?"

Now it is your turn to go silent. You leave and it takes every ounce of energy to not look back.

Rearview

THE PILOT LIGHT IS OUT AGAIN AND THIS TIME CRASH scrapes his tongue against the back of his teeth and on the roof of his mouth, making a sound that should have been more of an expression of frustration but ends up sounding like a fart.

You smile.

The kitchen counter is occupied by plates of cut broccoli and steak tips, diced onions and heaps of garlic freshly pressed and glistening like caviar in a porcelain bowl laced with sesame oil. Crash has promised to make lunch. Crash has also promised that Katrina would attend and yet he is alone in the apartment. You have told your in-laws you are meeting Katrina for lunch, and that you are getting all the details about her upcoming wedding.

"Get your infantile brain out of the bathroom joke book," Crash growls as he rummages through the drawer and, after a few moments, locates a box of extra long matches.

"I didn't say anything," you say.

You ask if you should set the table for three.

Crash shrugs, attempts to strike the match three times, and cannot get it to light. "You just want me to fail," he says.

"I'd rather not starve," you say, stomach grumbling. You find three of everything and lay them out on the table. You catch Crash looking at his watch, frowning. You stretch out your hand. "Can I try?"

He shakes his head. "No, I'll never live it down. I'm doing this, so go away."

You jump up to the bar stool seat. "I have to leave in an hour, an hour and a half tops."

He nods. "I just need the right vibe," and walks toward his wall of songs.

You and Crash argued over a song that led to his fighting words and door slamming, the skulking down the hall and out of the building. And now he's gone. You wonder how or where to start looking for him. In the old days you could guess where he would be after any fight between you: Merrick's, or the tree house at the very edge of the woods by the ravine, or the abandoned play set by the Baptist church, or tucked into an alcove at the community college library. But you are in the big city now, far away and worlds apart from Raleigh. Congestion on the roads, on the sidewalks, a busy weekday. In his car, he could be miles away by now. You brood in Crash's apartment and hope he'll return; you find the cassette in question, listen to "I Melt with You" even though Crash thinks the band sold out. You hope somehow that Katrina will arrive and then this entire situation can become her problem. You consult your watch again, you don't have long before you are tardy and your in-laws will ask extra questions, scold you. You put the meat in the fridge and decide to leave. Then you spy his car keys on a hook by the light switch and decide to try. He couldn't have gone far by foot.

First you drive his dad's Chevy down the two main boulevards that at one point briefly converge, and you perform the usual turns, three left turns followed by one right and then three right turns and then a left, until you traverse many blocks, and the streets begin to look the same, brightly colored awnings proclaiming Chinese food or Thai, an Italian bistro that you pass and then double back when you remember that Crash had talked about it casually as a place he liked to go drink espresso. The second time you drive by, you notice the details: dark, closed for lunch, and only open for dinner today, chairs piled atop the wooden tables, the bar empty, the bottles behind the counter full, and no one seated in the picture windows. Couples everywhere on the street, striding in step or languid as they hold hands and stop to window-shop, some women steering baby carriages, and you push your foot on the brake to slow down the car to get a closer look, maybe you will know someone and ask, maybe you could roll down your window and question a few trios of men talking and walking, maybe toward lunch at the bar and grill two stoplights away. A tall blond girl walks into the corner store and for a second you think it's Marie and almost slam the brake. But this girl comes out to look for someone and it's a stranger's face. You keep driving. Still no Crash. You drive in this way for a while, past the time the lunch crowds die down and workers return to their jobs, until it is almost happy hour. You know you should drive back to his apartment, replace the keys on the hook, and get back to your in-laws. Still you drive, knowing he couldn't have gone too far, even though the hours have crept by, stopping and starting at every intersection and every signal, waiting for the lights to turn green. You are turning east, toward his apartment, when you catch the light, the left turn arrow giving way to red too quickly. You glance at the clock on the dashboard and your heart thumps loudly.

You look in the rearview mirror and see Crash sucking face with a woman who is not his fiancée, that is to say, not Katrina, and then you are anchored firmly in the driver's seat, unable to look away and unable to keep looking, and yet you are doing both. You watch him behind you in an unfamiliar car, a buxom strawberry blonde leaning over the stick shift, kissing him with intensity.

Crash kissing back, his hands occupying the stick and black wheel of the shitty Honda. You shift your eyes from him to the woman occupying his affections, and back to him, your own breath shallow as you see his mouth on the other woman's, neck craned, eyes closed. You swear aloud. In the rearview you can see Crash, the way he is captive to this siren. The woman lets go and wipes the corner of his mouth with her finger, then tosses her hair and smiles the tiniest smile. Crash smiles at her the way he used to smile at you, when Marie was alive, and the woman takes her finger and wipes just under Crash's bottom lip. A volley of car horns behind you all, as the turn light changes from red to green.

Neither you nor Crash move.

You park the car in the turn lane, unfasten your seat belt, then push the hazard lights button. You want to scream, but instead force the air out of your lungs the way you once slashed Katrina's bicycle tires in the school parking lot after she'd made fun of your mother's sari. You leave the car running but step into the road and walk to the driver's side, intent on harm. The woman turns to concrete, rosebud mouth open, eyes glazing over. You can smell her perfume, and it is the same as your perfume, and you look closer, and that is your shade of lipstick, Havana Red, on her mouth, the blond rinse in the woman's hair not unlike the henna rinse in your own.

Crash bellows, "Jesus, Jesus," and quickly unbuckles, jamming his foot onto the clutch and putting the stick back into the resting position. He doesn't look back at his companion, but instead fixes a killer smile across his full lips, and gets out of the car.

"Hey, Dia," he says, his voice rising above the din of honking cars and passersby yelling, "What the hell are you doing?" and "You're going to get killed!" You are at once in New York and in Raleigh, outside Merrick's Farm.

You want to slap that face bloody and yank that bombshell out of the car by her hair. You can feel the heat of your own anger rise past your neck, inflaming your cheeks, shame at the notion that Crash might think you are blushing. You can almost feel your soul leave your body and run away. Your knees tremble.

With all of the bravado you have left within, you put your arms around his neck and draw your face close to his. Your eyes meet, and his eyes look exactly the same as they did hours before when you argued over Modern English in his apartment. You flex your feet upward and kiss him, tasting the other woman's cherry flavored lipstick.

Your first kiss if you don't count the one he stole at the water tower so long ago.

He returns the kiss for a moment then steps back.

You suck in your breath and drop your arms to your side, "Love her?"

Crash laughs aloud, a noise that begins in his belly, rises through his chest, and barrels out of his mouth as if he were delivering a tropical storm, wrecking the fragile coastline within you. How many more storms can you weather? He puts his fingertips at your waist as if to hold you in place, as if you both are going to ride out the swells and currents together.

Your eyes dart to the woman inside the car, and back to Crash's face, the laughter in his eyes, at the corners of his mouth.

The other woman comes to life. "Is this your wife?" she yells. "I thought you said your wife was dead."

Unexpected news

A COUPLE OF DAYS LATER, YOU THROW UP IN THE MORNING.
Just after you brush your teeth.

The test comes back: two blue lines.

Crossroads

CRASH CALLS YOU FROM A PAY PHONE, TELLS YOU HE AND Katrina eloped. "It was unexpectedly trite," he says. "You know, the whole Vegas-weekend-getaway-turned-wedding thing."

You picture Katrina and Crash at the slot machines, walking arm in arm under the blinking wattage of the Strip, at the Elvis Chapel. You picture your parents at the Grimaldis' wedding reenactment. "Should I offer my congratulations?"

Crash chuckles, sort of. "Not exactly. We didn't quite make it through the honeymoon."

You breathe in. "You're separating."

Crash groans his assent. "I was calling to tell you, you know, that I keep thinking about our kiss . . ."

You say you're sorry, you tell him his timing is terrible, you tell him you're expecting. A baby.

He gasps. Then: "I hope it's a girl."

You smile into the receiver. There is the hint of the Marco you remember. Here is a bridge between the past and the future. "Me too." You're going to name her Maitreyi, the name of a female saint in Vedic India, a name in modern times to mean "friendly," a name that holds Marie in it.

Interruption

WHEN YOU WALK INTO THE APARTMENT, THE THREE OF them are like birds clustered in the back of the living room by the picture window. The sun has set already, but the city still glows with life on the other side of the glass. Bright lights that continue to illuminate Neel and his parents as they step apart, their faces contorted in anger. Your in-laws are dressed casually, their after-hours home attire you've seen them put on when you know they won't be going out: black sweaters for them both and loose-fitting slacks, the kind that hang from the top poles at the shops in Little India. You set down your bag and drop your keys by the small table in the foyer and square your shoulders.

Your baby is a tight ball in your stomach and you can tell the baby is sleeping. You know your in-laws will be thrilled with a grandson, but you're hoping for a little girl. You stifle a yawn and look closely at Neel; this anger has flushed his face into an unhealthy flame, and you notice he's in a double-breasted suit and tie, his white shirt shimmering from the outside light. You put your hand on your stomach for a moment, and step toward them. You wonder if you've forgotten something, an invitation, an event. But you don't remember—the prenatal yoga class has left you sleepy and heavy, and you are looking forward to an early dinner and bed. You know they've seen you but this is the first time they do not stop at the sight of you. They continue for a few seconds longer:

whatever insult Neel has hurled at them, your father-in-law jeers and says, "I won't tolerate this!"

Neel yells in response, "No, no, no."

Your mother-in-law alternates between bewilderment and palpable pain, her finger frozen mid-wag.

It is as though they are crows fighting over some tasty scrap of food, something that is newly dead and still fresh.

You shiver.

Then your mother-in-law says, "Is it seven thirty already?"

You hiccup, then apologize. "Class let out early."

Your father-in-law welcomes you home, asks you to sit down, and volunteers Neel to bring you a drink and a snack.

You stand still as Neel picks up his key ring from the foyer table and walks past you, then slams the front door behind him.

Fog

YOU HEAR SOMEONE SHOUT FROM THE FLOOR ABOVE YOU. "My god, my god," the man repeats through walls, increasingly querulous as his wife or companion asks him what is wrong, unable to sputter the words out fast enough, unable to voice the horror of what he sees on the TV before him, as he turns up the volume.

You at home alone, nauseated and achy.

You stumble into your mother-in-law's bedroom, turn on the TV, the blood receding from your extremities, your hands and feet turning to cubes of ice, your eyelids growing heavy. You try to blink away the fog that descends, even though it is just after midday. It is not time to retreat to sleep.

The baby kicks.

The absence of sound is deafening in these moments when your thoughts recoil at the moving pictures on the screen: the emergency vehicles, swathed in flashing red lights, converging at the World Trade Center; the blood-soaked gurneys, firefighters and police frantic. They direct the response as thousands evacuate from lower Manhattan.

You tear your eyes away from the screen for a few seconds and images of Crash flood your mind: Crash stealing a kiss at the water tower; Crash at the airport baggage claim, waiting for you to come home before your wedding; Crash and Marie, the Tin Man and the Scarecrow; Marie promising Crash's safety for the next fifty years on the day of her death; Crash calling you the week before, telling you that he was going to look for other work since he and Katrina are splitting up, that he had an interview for a different firm at the World Trade Center. Today.

You look at the red ticker at the bottom of the screen.

An explosion.

The announcer repeating what the police said at first, perhaps strong February rains and lightning causing a reaction at the World Trade Center. The announcer coming back later: a car bomb in the subterranean parking garage of the hotel inside the tower, President Clinton due to address the nation in an hour. You stay still, unable to look away, unable to understand the moving pictures repeating every few minutes. You see Crash's face in your mind, you hear your own voice echoing, telling him not to rush, to put off the interview until his portfolio is in better shape. You hear him accuse you of not supporting him.

You look at the clock on your in-laws' nightstand.

It is still afternoon.

You cannot remember Crash's telephone number, you do not remember if he even has a phone at that studio, you do not remember the name of the building though you remember the street.

You rise with unexpected energy and your legs propel you out the bedroom door and down the hall quickly. You throw on your boots and your black coat and run out, keys in hand. You run six blocks and turn left and run another six blocks. Your chest contracts in pain as you breathe in and out the cold air.

The baby jiggles.

The keys jangle in time to your frantic beat.

Your hands stiffen and curl. You remember this pain from the day of Marie's funeral.

Eyes of strangers you pass on the street widen in surprise and curiosity. Eyes of strangers like buttons popping off different coats.

You arrive at his building on Van Kleeck Street. There is a strange silence, as if you're watching a movie with the volume muted. Your movements like a slow-motion dance as you slide on the tile in front of the elevator. The doorman is not at his post. The lobby is completely empty, as if there were no more people alive in the world.

Crash doesn't reply, first to the buzzer and then to your frantic knocks.

You run even faster back to your apartment.

Company

Y OU WALK INTO THE APARTMENT, MAKING A PLAN TO FIND Katrina's father's company name at the World Trade Center, to call them, to see if everyone is all right, to get Crash's whereabouts. But first you need to go to the bathroom: gestational incontinence.

Your mother-in-law looks you over. "Where have you been? You look terrible."

You freeze, try to answer—but she waves you off. "No matter. Your father-in-law has some guests coming for an impromptu dinner party. We must improvise."

You are sick at the thought of looking at food, you are sick at the thought of cooking. You want to find Crash. You are sick at the thought of Crash at the World Trade Center.

"I have to make a phone call," you say.

But she isn't listening. "He said just a few people, don't go to any trouble." Your mother-in-law shrugs. "I'm not a magician. And it's too late to call the caterer."

"Who are these people?" you ask, but she has already escaped to the kitchen.

You follow, and see she has bought a few things from the grocery store. "Did you see the news? I have to . . ."

Apparently she doesn't hear you. She points to the counter and steps toward the living room, ostensibly to fluff pillows.

You eye the phone but pick up the knife instead. You chop the vegetables coarsely, try to keep your heart from racing out of control. The anger rises inside you like a wave. You throw the new potatoes and carrots and parsnips into a roasting pan, see the chicken roasting in the oven, covered in tinfoil to keep it from turning dry. You try to blot out the pain that is emanating from your side. You put your pan to the side. You turn down the heat. Your mother-in-law has brown rice simmering on the stove and she comes back, reaches into her cabinet for the biriyani spices. Now is a good time for you to run into the study and use the phone. You also need to use the bathroom.

"I need to make a phone call," you say.

But she wants the large glass bowl for the salad of mixed greens, and asks you to fetch it. "Excuse me," she says, heading for her bathroom, and shutting the door to her bedroom behind her.

A pain stabs you in the stomach as you bend down. You stand, hands at hips, look at the clock and rule this out as a pang of hunger. The hurt shoots down from your pregnant stomach into your abdomen now. You call out to your mother-in-law, "Can you help me?"

"Don't worry about it," she says, voice muffled through the door. "Just do what you can, and I'll be out in a few minutes."

The toilet flushes, and the sink tap runs. The telephone rings. "I'll get that," your mother-in-law says.

You hear her coughing, laughing, crying? You wince in pain. She is speaking with your father-in-law. "Oh god," she exclaims. "Yes, of course."

"Please, I really need help," you say.

"Yes, yes."

Pain bursts forth, and you stand frozen, blood soaks your underwear and gravitates down your skirt. Some blood starts to pool at your feet and it is a lake, with a stone being skipped across, the waters disturbed and rippling outward. She tells her husband to cancel everything and come home, and the phone receiver is replaced into its black cradle.

"Bhagavan," she says when she opens the door. Her call to god is loud. The light is dim in the hallway, and casts a shadow on her face, over her pink top and white skirt. "How long have you been standing there?" After absorbing the bright red blood and recognizing the danger in that color and the pallor on your cheeks, the alarm enters her eyes: "Heera, why didn't you tell me?"

You open your mouth to answer, but instead groan in pain.

Your mother-in-law, voice soothing, says, "Let me call my husband. He can help."

You brace one hand against the frame of the wooden door. "I think I need a doctor first."

"Yes, yes, of course," she says, "I'll tell him to call Neel and meet us at the hospital."

She runs to the kitchen telephone and dials. "Yes, please send an ambulance. I think my daughter-in-law is going into an early labor."

She returns.

You point toward the kitchen.

"Don't worry about that now," she says. "The party got canceled. My husband told me about the explosion."

You shake your head and try to speak through your pain. "Need to turn it all off."

"Of course," she says, but makes no move toward the kitchen. The telephone rings instead.

You close your eyes as you slump forward, and the last thing you remember before the ambulance ride is your mother-in-law calling your parents. "Please meet us."

You are carried into the ambulance. The paramedic has eyes the color of a Caribbean sea, so blue, and you cannot look away. It is as though Marie's eyes are upon you. You stare at him and think of Crash. In the ambulance your mother-in-law holds your hand, her knuckles white; the sheet over your stomach scratchy, fluid oozing between your legs.

A jolt as the stretcher is lowered onto the ground, so much activity in the emergency room. People injured from the explosion are brought to this hospital because other medical centers are over-flowing. You hear shouting. A crisscross of fluorescent bars as you are wheeled into a room, a woman with a stethoscope urging the attendants to move faster and faster. Your mother-in-law some-where far behind waiting for your parents to arrive.

Awake

YOU COME OUT OF YOUR DREAM ABOUT A SLIP OF A GIRL IN A red cotton sari standing at the threshold of a door, beckoning you to enter. Khuku Roychowdhury, your great-aunt. The girl's face changes, and now before you it is the face of Krishna, static and smiling, the word MISSING above her head. You blink hard. You see Marie in a scarecrow's face. The sun floods the black and white squares of the hospital floor and the room is warmed. Ma dozes in a hard chair by the side of your bed, her hair an untidy bun, her arms folded, a hospital blanket thrown over her. Her lips are compressed, the corners bent downward.

Your husband is absent.

Your father and in-laws are nowhere to be seen.

You look down at your stomach and you know what the lack of movement means. You cry out, "No!"

Your mother jolts awake. "Sona, I'm sorry." She grabs your hand and squeezes it. "I'm so sorry."

You cry and cry, and she lets you, her one hand holding tight to your hand, her other hand patting your back.

"Son or daughter?" you ask in between sobs.

"Daughter," Ma says, softly.

"Maitreyi," you say, "for Marie."

After a while, you stop. You lean back and look at your mother. You can see from her face that she wants to say more.

"What? Tell me," you ask. "Where's Neel?"

She shakes her head. "We don't know."

You want to ask her, *Where's Crash?*

Boy, missing

NEEL MISSING BUT SO FAR NOT NAMED AMONG THE SIX dead, the thousand injured. From your hospital room bed, you help make phone calls, to hospitals and police precincts. Your parents are outside talking to the nurse, your in-laws are at their apartment, ostensibly calling friends and trying to find your husband, their only child.

Harried women and men saying "no, no one by that name here" each time you get past the minefield of busy signals and calls placed on almost-forever holds.

You ask about Crash as well. "Marco Grimaldi," you say, pressing your receiver to your ear, lowering your voice. "Is he on the list?"

The answers remain the same: no, no one by that name either.

Ma walks in as you sigh in relief and thank the woman on the line.

"What are you doing?" She takes the phone from your hand and replaces it in its cradle. "Why are you calling about Marco?"

You begin to explain, about the job interview.

Your mother puts her hand up. "Stop, Heera."

You ask why.

"What if your mother-in-law came in now, instead of me?" She shakes her head. "There is a time and place for everything. I know you are concerned about your friend, but first get your own house in order."

You wait until she excuses herself to use the restroom, then you pick up the phone and dial the operator, for the number of Crash's apartment building in Elmhurst. Van Kleeck Street.

You dial, and it rings and rings.

Finally, an answer.

You explain you are looking for Marco Grimaldi, on the third floor.

"Haven't seen him," the man says. He calls out to someone in the lobby, ostensibly the doorman. He pauses until he receives a reply. "No one's seen him."

Everyone appears as your discharge papers are being drawn up.

Everyone but Neel.

Your parents are tearful and your in-laws are strangely calm.

"I see her sometimes," you say to Baba as he helps you with your coat. "I see Khuku standing at the door."

Ma pales, but tells you to hush.

Baba buttons your coat, bites his lower lip. "We'd like to take Heera home with us for a while," Baba says to your in-laws a few minutes later.

The silence between you all is awkward and long. Your in-laws insist you come back to their apartment. "That's your home now," your mother-in-law says. "You're our daughter too." She squeezes your hand.

Ma wipes tears from her eyes, coughs.

"What will people say if we send you back to your parents at a time like this?" your father-in-law says. "We will take good care of you." He pats you on the shoulder.

Your mother-in-law leans in. "I'm still calling around on behalf of Neel. I'd love some help."

You nod and squeeze her hand in return.

You look at Ma and Baba and say, gently, "I'll come and visit."

They nod in unison.

Blood is thicker

EVERY DAY YOU VENTURE OUT FURTHER AND FURTHER, YOU are trying to out-walk your fear, you are trying to recover from the baby girl you lost.

The first week you stay on the same train line as your in-laws' apartment, just going down toward the city, and its center, neon lights even in the daytime beckoning people to come in and trade their gold, pawnshops with metal grills bifurcating the picture windows, massage parlors with signs that suggest their masseuses wear little more than a smile as they work.

By the end of the second week, you start to lift items from careless pedestrians you come across, the obvious tourists. You buzz buildings with no doorman until someone opens the door, and you take the elevator as far as it will go and climb to the rooftops. You take out your cheap camera and shoot the sidewalks in front of those glass-front buildings, catch the mirrored images as women walk by or a man stands at the curb and lights a cigarette. You favor solitary figures, reflections.

You swing by your parents' place and make sure they have food, Ma and Baba now in full retreat from their previous existence, barely venturing out of their apartment except to visit Ma's doctor.

You stop and go into meadows that are marked NO TRES-

PASSING. You slip through the fences, unlock the gates as Crash has taught you to do, and walk along the perimeter.

ɯ–ɯ

You walk and with every step you are closer to realizing your next dream. A couple more months, and you will have enough money saved from the steady pickpocketing to take the train north toward Canada. Once out of the city and its concrete skyline, you would breathe easy, the country would look like North Carolina this time of year: trees dark green, roads narrow, two-lane, wildflowers on the shoulders. You would start over somehow.

ɯ–ɯ

Another week. You walk and walk, and you find yourself at a street fair of sorts. Not the usual kind with tents of food cooking and artists selling handmade earrings, homemade jams, clothing. Tents, yes, but neatly arranged, at least two dozen, each with a large table and chairs. People darting from booth to booth, picking up brochures. You squint and notice the college pennants and signs looming behind people. An education fair. You look around and admire the buildings' architecture. You notice the cross street. You are at the outskirts of a community college. You stash your camera in your bag and walk up to a booth bearing the name of your university, the one you attended but had to drop out of.

A young woman in a blue blazer hands you a pen bearing the institution's name. "If you want some more information sent to your home, put your name down here."

You sign with your unmarried name and provide your parents' address, then slip the pen up your sleeve without thinking. "I'm a

former student," you say to the girl, whose eyes appear huge behind her pink-framed glasses.

"Welcome back," the girl says. "Wait here." She goes to the
rear of the tent and removes something from an opened cardboard
box. She returns and hands it to you. "This is the transitions office
brochure, you should call them if you want to return."

You thank her and move to another booth. Community college. A lady with long hair and a coat like your mother's hands
you a pamphlet. "Tuition is affordable and we have night classes
for students who hold jobs during the day," she says, flashing very
straight teeth. After a short while, you come across a booth shared
by several universities. You learn they belong to the same athletic
conference including Temple, Villanova, East Carolina, and Tulane. You think of Krishna, and ask for the Tulane brochure.

You hold a glossy magazine in your hand, images of stately
buildings and green grass, students congregating on a main avenue on campus, professors giving lectures in giant auditoriums, a
glamorous shot of Bourbon Street and downtown New Orleans at
night, lights twinkling everywhere. You sit down at a table, and
look through every photo, your breath catching Krishna's name in
your throat. On a page of alumni, last year's graduates congregate
on a sloping lawn, groups clustered in caps and gowns with arms
slung over each other's shoulders beaming into the camera. You
stop at the photo on the second to last page, a dark-haired girl with
several strands of Mardi Gras beads roped over her graduation
gown, standing with her mother, an alumna of the same university, at the crossroads of campus. You don't recognize them, but
you envy their moment of triumph. You read the caption underneath and learn both mother and daughter are also sorority sisters
—and realize this photo is a year old.

Behind the right shoulder of the mother, in the distance, a

tree bears its many thousand leaves, and at its base rests a stone bench. There you spot a familiar form, face in silhouette, a camera in her hand, blue slacks, navy blouse. You stare at the body holding the camera, poised to lift it up to her eye and shoot. You wish for a magnifying glass, you wish to jump into the photograph and run toward her. You turn the page and force yourself to look at something else, just to refocus. Eventually, you turn back and study the image again. You are all but certain it is Krishna.

Your first impulse is to find a pay phone and call Ma and Baba. Standing, you sling your backpack over your shoulder, searching for signs to the nearest subway station. You take a few steps and look down at the glossy magazine. You stop. You think back to Anjuli's demeanor on the news. *She knows. She knows her didi is alive.*

You look back at the education fair, and think. You shuffle through the stack, find the brochure for the city college; look at the black-and-white of a teacher at the chalkboard, students raising their hands; on the next page, you spy photojournalism among the listed majors. You memorize the number for admissions. For now, instead of Canada, you could take a local train and disappear in to the biggest city in America, rent a room, take classes, find a way to graduate.

You find the nearest trash can and throw everything away.

↳↲

One Tuesday in June you step out of the bedroom to find your sneakers and get some change out of the Rocky Road container in the freezer. It is where you hide the money; your health-conscious mother-in-law balks at dessert. Then you hear a key in the lock. You quickly take off your windbreaker and stuff it and your back-pack behind the settee in the living room. Your mother-in-law comes in, startled to see anyone at home. "Oh, I didn't know you'd be here," she says. "I was just coming to check on you, you seem to disappear this time every week."

You see that she has spilled mustard on her tailored silk blouse. "Just going for a walk," you say.

The air is pungent: she smells of raw onions and cinnamon mints.

"But you go every week at the same time," Neel's mother says. "Do you meet friends?"

You picture Crash, the last time you saw him. Just for a moment. "I don't have any friends in this city," you say.

Your mother-in-law purses her lips. She does not believe you.

In the time you were at the hospital, she replaced your ward-robe with widow-white clothes. White slacks, white blouses, bleached wide-leg jeans. She slated your clothes for the donation truck, but you managed to take back a few things and hide them in the space between your mattress and box spring. She steps closer, and sniffs, checking for alcohol. Your father-in-law did the same thing the other day, checking your pockets for evidence of ciga-rettes. They squint and touch the shades of red you infrequently use to tint your lips, a spot staining their index fingers after the inspections. "You want to wear lipstick, with Neel missing?" The first time your mother-in-law says it you're torn between shame and anger.

Now you've become one of those girls who puts on makeup in the elevator on the way out of the building. "I have no friends here," you say, remembering how you ran toward Crash the day of the bombing, the miscarriage, remembering how you regularly call the apartment building manager and he has replied in the same way for the past two and a half months: "Haven't seen him."

She clasps her hands together. "What will people say if they see you out with friends, at this time?" she asks.

"All I do is walk," you say, and try to step around her.

She puts a hand on your bundled arm. She wants you to stay home and mourn his absence. So they can still move about in their circles without ostracism, so they can claim closure.

All you want is to be alone, not physically alone, not like a hermit in a cave or a hut thousands of miles away from civilization. No, you want to be left alone from the well-meaning neighbors who are the in-laws' acquaintances and from your in-laws too, everyone always checking on you, with any excuse: "I thought I heard something," one of them would say, "Can I come in?" Or "I need to borrow some eggs. It's for an emergency omelet." Or "Can you please go get the super? There's a dead mouse behind the fridge, and the phone's on the wall in the kitchen." You just want to be alone, a few minutes every day without people eyeing you and wary of your every move. "I won't be long," you say, breaking free.

"This is so unlike you, Heera," she calls after you.

You are leaving the lobby when one of the neighbors stops you. The lady on the floor above, who came over to borrow an egg. "Heera, the mailman put your mail in my box. I'm embarrassed to say this was some time ago. Can you please take it, and give it to your mother-in-law? And apologize to her?"

You say yes, and she hands you an envelope. The phone bill. "Thank you," you say to each other, and you tuck it into your pocket, walk out the glass doors.

You find a pay phone far from your in-laws' neighborhood. You call the city college, and ask about their deadlines.

"It's rolling admissions," says the man on the other end of the line. "I can mail you an application, or you can come to us and pick up in person."

Hours later, you return to an empty apartment. You turn on the lights and look around for a note but find none. You take off your windbreaker and remember the envelope in your pocket. You open it and look through the pages and pages of numbers. Some you recognize as your in-laws' friends, and others appear to be business calls to the West Coast. You study the local numbers and decide to let these last people know Neel is presumed missing. Your mother-in-law has suffered enough making hundreds and hundreds of calls.

The first number you try is a hospital outside of the city. "Sorry, miss, you'll have to call back when the records department opens in the morning."

The second number is a pharmacy. "I'm calling to inform you that my husband has been missing since February . . ." you begin.

The voice on the other end takes down Neel's information. "I'm sorry for your loss. I'll let the pharmacist know tomorrow."

The next two numbers are area clinics, and neither is open.

The last number is a residence. A woman answers.

"I'm calling to inform you that my husband has been missing since February . . ." you begin again.

The woman listens until you are finished. "I'm so sorry for your loss," she says.

You hear two distinct voices in the background but cannot discern what they are saying. "Are you a friend of my husband?" you ask.

"Our family has known yours for years, since college," she says. "My family wanted me to offer you their condolences."

"Thank you." You want to ask her so many questions, instead your throat starts to close. "I have to . . . go," you say, not knowing whether to say thank you or goodbye.

"Hello?" the woman asks. "Are you still there?"

"Goodbye," you choke out, then hang up.

ॐ

Another week flies by, then two, your in-laws begin answering the phone in the bedroom or the study, always closing the doors behind them. Your father-in-law goes out one day, ostensibly for groceries, and returns hours later, empty-handed. Your mother-in-law begins to spend more time in her room, watching TV. She goes out in the afternoon, to see friends. She returns, eyes rimmed red, cheeks swollen from a squall of tears.

ॐ

The telephone rings, and your father-in-law answers.

"It's for you," he says, handing you the sleek black receiver. There is sadness reflecting from his eyes, and resolve in the way his jaw is locked.

You hold your breath for a second, to calm what feels like caterpillars crawling inside your stomach. You hear the voice on the telephone. And you hold your breath again as the voice speaks calmly, asking you questions that only require a yes or a no. After a moment, you exhale and answer monosyllabically. You look hard at your mother-in-law and she cannot hold your gaze.

You don't say goodbye when the call ends, you merely ask for their car keys.

They seem unsurprised at the request.

Your father-in-law hands over the keys without a word.

Your mother-in-law stands up from the couch suddenly as if she was going to accompany you, but sits down again.

You want to call your parents but first you must be armed with answers. First you must unravel this terrible riddle. Otherwise, you will not be able to stomach their questions, their disappointment, their hurt. You want to call Crash, but he has disappeared from the only place you knew him to be. You are afraid to call his mother, you want to believe the best, that he is safe somewhere, that he is not dead. It is better not to know than to witness another great loss, arguably the greatest loss since Marie's death. You do not think you can handle one more thing and yet you borrow your in-laws' car and follow the directions set forth in the phone call moments before.

You drive for a while, to a small park near a library in the suburbs. You try the radio, for company, but every song is a love song and you cannot sing along today. The silence inside the car is a punch to the side of the head but you cannot break that silence. You park the car in the visitors' lot, rub your hands together for warmth, then step out of the car. Your abdomen is still sore with phantom pain. The last vestige of your failed pregnancy.

Neel emerges, his eyes covered by sunglasses though the sky is overcast. He stops on the sidewalk in front of you and spreads his hands out in a gesture of helplessness. He takes off the sunglasses and dangles them in his hand.

"Where have you been?" you ask, surprised at the anger in your voice. You do not love him, but still, this act of vanishing is cruel. Haven't you been through enough? You are on the cusp of twenty-four and yet you've lived a lifetime. How many more losses? Your husband presumed dead for six months and yet he stands before you. All of your old losses come back to haunt. Marie. Your separation from Crash. How your parents are in the same city with you and yet you can't break free of your in-laws to see them.

You are so conscious of the time and the relationship to date, another birthday looming, another year where you feel Marie's absence sharply, and this year your baby girl's absence too. You are certain of nothing but this moment, another Saturday in the late summer of 1993. Your dead but not dead husband stands before you, before trees begin their final change. In his own way, he is begging for forgiveness, hoping you'll continue to cover for him. He is just like his parents, who are also hoping you'll continue to live the lie Neel birthed so that they can hold their heads up in public, so that they can say their son was not a coward and a liar.

"Sarah's family has a place not far from here," he says, closing the arms of the sunglasses and putting them in his jacket pocket.

The sun peeks out from behind dense clouds and for a moment the world is lighter.

You shake your head. You have so many questions, and even more accusations. And yet you've known for a while, haven't you? That there was a body to go with the voice he spoke to in the middle of the night? That he wasn't dead? That someone else had grabbed hold of his heart? "Am I the last one to know?"

He pauses, nods. "I've loved her since college."

You remember the voice on the telephone. The woman you called who said in her kind voice that she'd known Neel for years. "If I had done this to you, you wouldn't have stood for it." It's still a man's world where the rules diverge. You run your hand through your hair.

"I have been thinking about family a lot," Neel says, speaking carefully, slowly, "and I'm here because my family asked me to come and talk to you."

You stare at him and see something new in his eyes. His gaze is direct and clear, as if a terrible weight has been lifted. "Since when have you cared what your parents want?"

"Not them. Sarah."

The sky behind him is your favorite shade of blue. "I am your family too," you say, holding up your wedding band. "You could have told me any time before the wedding, you could have told me any time even after we started sharing a bed."

His head snaps back as if you'd struck him across the face. "I'm sorry." He steps toward you, puts his hand on your stomach, now flat. "I'm so sorry about your . . . our . . . baby."

You feel your face harden. You can't cry in front of him, Neel is not worth your tears. Even in this moment, because this is the first moment that he has shown you any compassion, the first moment that he has acknowledged your existence. "Did they tell you about our baby girl?"

He nods. "Once you feel better . . . what . . . what are you going to do?"

You want to tell him but you don't know his intentions. "I suppose you're coming back with your . . . family."

He shakes his head. "My life is here with Sarah, and with Kevin."

And suddenly you know. The answer that answers all of the questions. But still, you ask. "Kevin?"

The corners of his mouth turn upward. "My son."

You know and yet you gasp.

He is a father and you are not a mother.

A marriage riddle. Now solved.

"Does Sarah's family know about . . . Kevin? Do they know about me?"

Neel nods, they were told when he was born. "It helped that our son was healthy and happy. They were very angry but when they saw him . . . overall, they have behaved decently."

You hear the word *decently* and you don't know whether to laugh or cry. You open your mouth and "well, that's something" comes out. You cry, and stumble back to your in-laws' car.

He follows you. "I'm sorry," he says. "I'm so sorry."

You turn around, uncaring now whether he sees your tears or hears your anger. You notice him fumbling with the sunglasses again, then returning them to his face. "Were you going to let me have the baby and have Sarah on the side?"

"I . . . I don't know," Neel says. "When the bombing happened, everything . . . everything became simple. I couldn't live with their expectations. I couldn't miss another minute of Kevin's life."

You stare and stare at his face, at his mirrored sunglasses.

౼౼

You drop the car keys into your father-in-law's outstretched hand. "How long have you known, Mr. Acharya?"

"He's my son."

"How long?"

He doesn't reply.

"I'm leaving," you say.

Your mother-in-law comes out of her room. "No no, what will people say? We will never be able to show our faces again."

You can't help but smile. "Not because of me, Mrs. Acharya."

Your father-in-law says, "I cannot accept what my son did. But he is my son."

"Yes," you say. "He is your cowardly son."

Your father-in-law sputters like the engine of an ancient automobile.

Your mother-in-law tells her husband to be quiet. She grabs ahold of your hand. "Please, don't leave. Please, we will work something out."

But you break free and go into your bedroom, shut the door. You retrieve vestiges from your previous life from under the mattress and begin to pack.

Embers, in Hindi

ALTHOUGH THE TENEMENT LOBBY IS DEVOID OF LIFE, SOMEone on the upper floors has *Sholay* going at full volume. You know exactly where it is in the movie that came out six years after you were born, in fact: the moment Amitabh Bachchan first states his intentions toward the young woman, as she fiddles with oil lamps on the balcony. In his real life, Amitabh had already married the actress, perhaps without his family's blessing. In the film, the woman was already a widow and could not remarry. The music is wistful and you remember how the real life couple stood admiring each other's beauty, something they could not touch there on the silver screen. As Amitabh spoke to the girl, you hear a neighbor woman on the third floor complain, "Yeah, why don't you ever talk to me like that Amitabh? I would have married you no matter what."

From an adjacent apartment, a door opens and a voice replies, "God, it must be Tuesday. You're having your fantasies about living in Bombay with Amitabh again, Mrs. Sharma. Do turn it down."

"It is a free country, here, Mr. Chowdhury," says the woman, her voice shrill. "I can watch Amitabh anytime I like."

"But I shouldn't have to suffer your freedoms," he says, before slamming the door.

The volume shrinks but only until the villain arrives, by horse. You mouth the rogue's words of warning to Amitabh Bachchan, cautioning him to stay away and not interfere with fate. The music reaches its crescendo, and Mrs. Sharma says, "Arey, he's so bad. How can I love him if he's so bad?"

Light from the windows above the lobby doors now glare strong and hot, warming the stagnant air. Your stomach rumbles as you open the mailbox with your key, papers spilling on your legs and onto the dirty tile. Flyers for pizza, *buy 1 get 1 free*, and plumbing improvement offers, the second notice from Con Ed, this time with a reminder—*Your attention is required! Time sensitive!*—stamped on the front. An envelope with familiar handwriting scrawled on the front, addressed to you, with your married name on it. You pause to check where you are, in your parents' building, on a weekday, your suitcase in tow, stopping in to make tea, and tell them about Neel, and tell them about your plans to leave for good. Community college a lighthouse in the distance. A turbaned driver sounds his cab horn as he skims the street, Bally Sagoo blaring from his rolled-down windows; pairs of men in pencil-cut pants black as their coconut-oil slicked hair, jabbering as they crowd the sidewalk. Jackson Heights at midday.

The envelope has tiny writing on the bottom: *do not bend, please cancel by hand.* Something solid but thin, something rectangular stationed inside.

On good days your father ventures as far as the lobby and the mailbox, but your mother has rarely left the bedroom and its girded view of the narrow courtyard and the people who live in the next building. They do not go far. Doctor's office, but nowhere else. Not since the car bomb at the World Trade Center, not since you lost the baby and your in-laws wouldn't let you go home. You haven't been by in almost a week, and the envelope could have been waiting for you in the intervening time.

You stoop to pick up the mail and stuff most of it into the side pocket of your satchel. You lock the box, one final tug, and find a place to lean against the railing of the staircase. Mr. Chowdhury exits his apartment. You hear him bolt his door and descend the curved steps. You wait until he walks by you. A crumpled old man in a suit made in India going out to the kebab palace for lunch. He asks, "Back again?"

You usually say yes and smile. Today, embedded in his question is a patronizing tone. What if this was the one thing you could change today? What if you didn't try to please him, an aloof neighbor who never cares to check on your parents? You close your mouth and don't answer.

He leaves the building but not before he turns his head, surprise in his eyes.

You absorb his expression and smile a little.

You look at the envelope and then at the staircase. You sigh at an OUT OF ORDER sign that has been posted on the elevator, hastily taped and crookedly positioned, for months. You trudge up the stairs, past the landing that leads to Mr. Chowdhury's apartment, and up one more flight past Mrs. Sharma. You listen to the music and know Amitabh Bachchan and his sidekick are hiding behind a boulder at this point; only the audience can see them. Amitabh and sidekick are watching the girlfriend dance on broken glass to entertain a whole band of thieves and marauders with her lip-synced Bollywood number and tight red bodice — and wondering how to rescue her. You reach the top floor and stop to find the correct key on the ring. The door swings open and Baba peers out of the frame. "What took you so long? Did you get the mail?" He looks at the suitcase for a long time before reaching for the handle and bringing it inside.

*

The apartment smells of gassy antiseptic cream that came out of a tube and no doubt expired years before; and of mealy bread lingering over the vanilla scented incense that burns night and day in a clay bowl in front of the altar to Saraswati, the goddess of learning. Baba's favorite.

You look closely at Baba as he steps out of the dim hallway and into the bedroom, spots of cream covering places on his cheek and neck that he cut shaving. Stacks of books and periodicals sprout from the floor like a tree, and half-drunk cups of black tea congeal on the nightstand. Dramatic music pierces the curtained room through the drywall as Amitabh Bachchan lies bleeding while his dost, his friend who led him into the preceding gunfight, proclaims his admiration for Amitabh, thanks him for taking the bullet.

Your mother waits. "It's too much," she says, and pulls the lime green terry cloth shroud more tightly over her face, her prayer book on her pillow. "I can't do this anymore."

Usually you mime concern, bring her a fresh cup of tea, adjust a blanket over her frail frame, perform a mock scolding to Baba for maintaining his wake-before-dawn custom and forcing Ma to have tea when all she wanted was more time to dream. But for the first time, you don't pause. "We've all been doing this for the past five plus years, Ma," you say. Your own voice surprises you, how tired you sound, how tinny. The two of you play a game of post office that should have ended years ago but still the message is bouncing back and forth. You remember a few lines of Mary Oliver and you say them aloud, ending with *"the soft animal"* of the body giving itself permission to love.

Ma's wail is muffled, but the words are as sharp as a new pair of scissors, slicing through the sour air of the apartment. "Even now, you only care for yourself, and that boy. You don't even see past him."

Baba stands like a garden statue, the kind that seems poised for flight but only spouts recycled water through a blackened mouth.

"The boy has a name," you say. "In fact, he stopped being a boy years ago. You saw what was happening, and you didn't stop to help." It is always the same images framing your mind: Marco, before he proclaimed himself Crash, standing next to the medic, his face awash in sorrow, then his sister, your best friend, carried away by the ambulance. The police lights flashing across Marco's face as if he were at a disco.

"That boy had no sense," Ma says.

You want to say something nasty, about Neel. But you are fresh out of words.

Baba picks up the TV remote and the midday news flickers on-screen. He turns down the volume so that the carefully coiffed man sitting in the chair is miming the words, and occasionally dispensing a wry yet strangely empathetic smile. Baba asks, "What kind of man was he going to be, growing up with those parents? How could I in good conscience have you waste your life on him?"

You want to hurl the framed black-and-white photograph of your maternal grandparents standing in front of the Victoria Memorial from the nightstand and splash the tea onto the wall, you want to drag Ma and Baba to their bathroom mirror and force them to see themselves, you want to show your real face to them, the lips that never smile without purpose, the eyes that only leak tears when you are alone. *Look how I turned out,* you want to scream. *I'm no different. I am identical to him in almost every way.* Instead, you dig your nails into the palms of your hands. "Marco. His name is Marco."

At the sound of his actual name, Baba turns up the volume on the remote in time to hear the anchorman say, ". . . a thirteen-car pileup on the expressway. More on that crash at the bottom of the hour."

You hold your breath for a long moment and will yourself not to flinch as Ma and Baba look at each other.

"Crash." Your mother pulls the terry cloth off her face. "Has he called you?"

"No," you intone. "I haven't seen or heard from him since the bombing."

Your father mutes the TV again.

You barrel across the room, then yank the remote out of Baba's hand and throw it over your shoulder. "I want you to say his name," you hiss as the remote lands with a thud on the floor. "His real name."

Baba shrinks back a little but stands a foot away from you, still. "What good will come from this?"

You toss the stack of bills onto the bed.

"You are a married woman," Ma says. "Even now." She struggles to sit up in the bed, lime green terry cloth around her like sea foam.

"Am I?" you ask. The envelopes land together with hardly a sound, and the one on top is the second notice from Con Ed.

Your father looks at you for a while. "You know something."

And you tell them, about Neel, and his longtime girlfriend and their little son. The words spill forth uncontrollably. You cry again. You end with your in-laws' plan, how they want you pretend that you're a widow so they don't have to tell their friends that their son has run away, that he has abandoned them.

Baba turns off the TV, mumbles a Sanskrit prayer.

Ma closes her eyes for a long second. "That's not all," she says.

"Isn't it enough?" you ask, but something in your voice quivers like an arrow straying off course. "I wanted to talk to you about staying here," you say.

Ma and Baba look at each other. The mood in the room shifts. "Of course," she says, smiles. The wrinkles on her face vanish.

"As long as you want," Baba says.

You exhale loudly, in relief. "Just until I figure things out."

Ma sits up. "Did you give me everything?"

You remember the envelope, take it out.

She points to it.

"This?" you ask. "What is this?"

Baba sits down at the foot of the bed and looks into the dark screen of the TV, mouthing something that you could not quite hear, something about the other.

"You've hidden my mail?"

"You are married," Ma says, saying that she'd written *return to sender* on the other envelope that had come in the past two months. But she shouldn't have bothered, there was no return address on it anyway.

It doesn't matter that you agreed to an arranged marriage, that you miscarried, that your husband was among the missing since the bombing, that you found out that he was a liar and the father to a baby boy, that you held your composure and your tongue in front of your husband's parents, that your best friend had died and that her one sibling in the world was most likely gone: it didn't matter, because your parents still saw you as the rebellious teenager you once were.

Your mother throws over the robe and the bedspread, and covers the mail in a tsunami of cloth. She yawns, then swings her thin legs over the side of the bed—stretches her arms out toward you as if she were reaching for a baby.

You hand it over, the envelope, and your mother tears open the top and empties out the contents onto the unmade bed.

A piece of paper, yellow and legal sized, you judge from the way it is folded and refolded to fit its container, a pirate's patch presumably from an old Halloween costume and a photo, dog-eared and faded. Years ago, before Marco became Crash, he left you letters in the mailbox. They were blank. Yellow meant for you to meet up at the water tower after your parents had retired to their bedroom for the evening. But there are too many water towers in New York, and the handwriting on the envelope is not Crash's or, at least, not the handwriting you remember. Your mother picks up the photo and surprise swims across her face—she holds it up to you. "Who are these boys? And where are you?"

You snatch the photo from her. A few kids, arms around each other's shoulders, smiling into the camera eye, you on the left as Dorothy in a borrowed gingham dress and Marie in the middle as the Scarecrow, blond tresses hidden under a hat, breasts hidden under her dad's plaid flannel shirt, face hidden by theatrical paint. Another girl on the right dressed as a pirate, a patch over one eye, and a cardboard sword covered in foil at the ready. Katrina. Marco in the background as the Tin Man, an oilcan in one hand. You remember there was vodka in that can that night.

You want to keep that photo and hug it tightly to your chest. You want your heart to stop hurting so much. You want to take the photo and go outside and study it in the light, with the noise of New York around you, bhangra thumping in the distance, women dressed in their colorful best, vermillion powder in the part of their braided hair, talking and laughing and eating all around you, alive.

Ma asks again, "Who are these people you are with?"

The silence hangs in the air like a giant unseen cloud ready to unleash rain. It was the day of your greatest heartbreak, and you are sad that your mother cannot remember. "Just friends," you say, "it was a long time ago."

Your mother's stare is awash with disbelief. "You look exactly the same. This could have been taken last week."

You smile. "It's very old," you say, "those girls are long gone."

Baba stands up and then comes to where Ma sits, picks up the patch and tosses it to you. You catch it and your hand closes over it like an oyster protecting its black pearl.

Ma looks at Baba.

Baba mouths something, and Ma says again, "That's not all."

She opens her prayer book and pulls out the photo, of her with Mr. Grimaldi and his first wife. "I want to tell you . . ."

You look at her, the precious souvenirs of your past in hand, and apologize. Twice.

She nods and opens her mouth but no sound escapes.

"Ma, why don't we visit your old friends? Get you out of here for a few hours?"

She shakes her head slowly. "I don't have any friends here."

"Sure you do," you say, nodding at the photo. "Mr. Grimaldi's wife, first wife."

Ma shakes her head. "I can't visit her."

"Why not?"

Her mouth bends down then opens with a thin moan. "I don't know where she's buried."

And then you finally learn the story behind the photo of the Grimaldis. Sophia had not wanted children, she had not wanted to leave New York and her ailing mother. These are the facts you knew. Ma had tried to talk to her friends, counseled them not to give up on their marriage so easily.

And when Mr. Grimaldi could not convince his first wife on either count, he'd left her, called a lawyer.

"They were in the middle of their divorce, and it was so terrible, all of their fights. They lived just down the hall from us. One day she left work after lunch, she worked in a little office above a bookstore or a printing press. She didn't come over for dinner like she was supposed to," Ma says now, her voice as far away as her memory. "Next day, there's a policeman at my door, telling me she was in a terrible car accident on the turnpike and that she was gone."

And just like that, Ma says, Mr. Grimaldi was remarried, with Marco already on the way, and Marie not far behind. Technically, he was a widower, and he could remarry in the church. "He carried on, as if nothing had changed," she says, then coughs. "He never looked back."

But you remember his face after Marie's death, flushed and wet with tears. You also remember how he wanted to dismantle his daughter's room and end the constant reminder of death. "We have no idea what's going on with him. We shouldn't judge," you say, echoing Marie, remembering how she fixed Katrina's pirate sash in the bathroom.

"I tried for so many years," Ma says, "to be friends, but in the end I . . . couldn't let her go."

Return of the pickpocket

YOU KNOW WHAT YOU ARE, A PETTY THIEF. A PICKPOCKET. An astoundingly good one, even after all of these years. Tubes of lipstick, billfolds of course, money clips, candies wrapped in cellophane. Whatever you can slip from other people's coat pockets into yours, practicing a bit of magic, making something disappear from one place and reappear in another. You haven't lost your soft touch, even though you haven't had time to practice regularly.

When you practice you think of him.

You think you hear him for a moment in the library in the reference section, talking to the desk librarian on duty—you think you hear Marco's low laughter, in response to a flat joke. He always acknowledged even the poorest attempts at humor, he appreciated the effort. You turn around to get a better look, you search through the stacks, but find yourself hunting for a ghost.

Reunion

W HEN THE DOORBELL RINGS YOU ARE ALREADY AT YOUR
mother's sink, putting down the teacup and its chipped
saucer, wiping your hands at the hem of the faded yellow dish-
rag folded neatly into a square. You turn your eyes away from the
photograph in the copy of *National Geographic* that lies open on
the counter. "I'll get it," you say to your parents' unmoving forms.
They are statues, not unlike the photograph of the family sitting
at the table in Pompeii when a shower of gas and ash from the
volcanic eruption immortalized them without warning.

You are all up early. It is moving day for you — you have found
a furnished room near the community college. Baba wants you
to have your own place but Ma wants you to stay and study from
their apartment. You will try it, this rented room and your parents'
tether. If it all fails, you will flee to Canada and start over. Plan
C. You haven't told your parents about the possibility of Montreal
or maybe Toronto, you hold these hopes like pearls, close to your
heart. You carry your passport in the inside pocket of your backpack, a tangible secret.

Ma whispers through unmoving lips, "I can't imagine anyone
coming at this hour." It is too early, morning. You wonder for a
second as you turn the knob, if it is your father-in-law coming to
fetch you, try to convince you to return to their apartment. You are

tired, though you have had many hours of sleep. Always the same dreams: Khuku Roychowdhury standing at the doorway, then you are running as fast as you can but you can never catch up to Marie —she remains close to the horizon, a shadow blocking out the setting sun. You have stopped dreaming of Krishna. You want to share with Baba but it is still too soon to tell him.

You open the front door and find Crash leaning up against the wooden frame. "You have no idea how many people I had to bribe to get your address," he says, a smile in each eye.

Your breath catches at the back of your throat. "I don't live here," you say too quickly. Your mouth parched and your palms rapidly damp. You stare. He looks like his father, the young Mr. Grimaldi in the photograph Ma has kept for more than two decades.

"Is that the first thing you're going to say to me?" he asks.

You want to draw him close, take in the aftershave, and touch the salt that glistens prematurely in the pepper of his wavy hair. You want to scream at him for making you believe that he might be dead for all of these months. Instead you gulp. "I have to close the door now."

Then Crash straightens himself and stands to his full height, a grin rippling to the outer edges of his face. "You're not going to invite me in?"

You stare at his mouth for a second too long. "This isn't my home anymore."

A body behind you comes to life. "Who is it, Heera?"

Even now, Ma won't acknowledge your name, the name you have had ever since Marie died. Even now, Ma won't acknowledge your enduring sadness.

Crash crosses his arms and rocks a little on the balls of his feet. "How is she?" he asks, his voice dropping to a gossipy whisper. "Has she missed me?"

You bite the inside of your cheek to keep a straight face. "I promised her I'd never see you again." You shake your head for a moment.

"Promises like that . . ." he says as he spreads out his hands in front of you, "are meant to be broken."

You do the same, spread your hands like a fan. You both wear wedding bands.

"Heera? Is it the milkman, finally?"

His band contains ridges on the outer side like the edge of an ocean as it reaches a shoreline, and then you look down at your own, a perfect match. "We picked the same rings," you say, then chuckle.

"It's a sign," Crash answers.

Your eyes sting a little at first and then you smile to yourself that you're both the same kind of human, wearing wedding rings even after the marriages are over. You're both the same kind of human, hopeful but slow to change.

"Don't stand in the doorway," Baba calls out. "There's a draft. Go out to the hallway or invite your guest in."

Crash's eyes are twin snowcapped peaks on a cloudless day they are so bright. He mouths the word *guest*.

But you shake your head. No. "I cannot ever let you inside this door."

"But he invited me." His hand is on yours and they stick together as if glued. Your heart beats so fast you believe it will run away.

He steps inside, drops his backpack to the ground, and you shut the door behind him. You hear the chair legs squeak and your parents move, rise from the table and walk out of the kitchen. You hear Baba's breath turn into a lingering cough, the kind that won't disappear for another three months and Ma's increasingly voluminous exclamations in Bengali: "My god, my god. How could you invite Marco here, Heera? How could you let him back into our lives? Is that why you came here?"

You are grateful Ma's outburst is not English. But Crash knows this tone. You wait for Crash to defend himself, offer an apology for disturbing your parents so early in the morning, and deny aloud that you have lured him there. Instead he lingers in the tiny foyer, his eyes affixed on the glossy eighteen-by-twenty-four wedding photo hanging on the front wall in a gilded frame that is wearing thin at the corners. Portrait of a bride, standing in an empty room. Alone.

Baba continues to cough and Ma's voice becomes louder than the groan of the air-conditioning unit, gasping and moaning as it stops and starts. White noise, a constant pattern repeating itself and presenting nothing new. At first you wait for Ma to stop yelling, and then wait for Baba's coughs to subside, and then wait for Crash to stop staring at the bejeweled copy of your face and look at the real girl. But nothing changes, they continue on their own paths, together in one room again but each alone. In the old days before your marriage, your parents would not turn away any guest at the door, there was always a welcome proffered, however awkward the moment or the lateness of the hour.

You meet Ma's eyes and put a finger to your own lips. Baba's coughs subside. Your mother abruptly sits down, in a chair across from your father.

Crash finally looks at you, sadness dulling his eyes. You say to him, "Please sit down with them, I'll make some more tea."

Crash takes a chair with no back cushion as you scurry into the kitchen and put water in the kettle.

"How do you take your tea these days?" you ask.

No one speaks.

You open the fridge but find nothing suitable to eat, last night's leftover chicken in an airtight container with a bright red lid staring back at you. No rice. A pot of orange marmalade rests alone on the shelf in the fridge doorway, but no bread anywhere. You spy a half carton of eggs and a wedge of red onion wrapped in plastic behind your parents' considerable medicines that require refrigeration. "How about an omelet?"

Still nothing.

You cannot stand still, you cannot sit down, you cannot control the sudden tremors in your hands. You calm yourself by moving about the spare room, pushing in the kitchen chairs with their yellow vinyl backs so they are tucked under the tabletop, carrying your parents' teacups to the counter next to the stove—and placing them next to the good mug you have taken out of the cupboard for Crash. You open the cupboard and get one more cup for yourself but then put it back.

In a cabinet, you find a package of cream crackers, already opened—you put a corner in your mouth and taste the musty air of the kitchen. You put it on the snack plate anyway.

The kettle whistles.

"I take it black," Crash calls out.

"Like your heart," Ma says in Bengali to no one in particular.

They drink in silence and you watch.

You remember your last conversation, the threat of returning to Raleigh permanently. You ask, "Are you here for good?"

"I think so." His voice low and steady like the hum of the fluorescent beam in the next room. "I got the job."

You ask him if it's the job he'd been preparing for in February. Ma's glance at you is a shard of glass.

"I couldn't go empty-handed, with my portfolio in such bad shape," he says, his voice quiet. "You taught me that."

You nod. "Everything okay at home?" You should be enraged at him for not telling you that he was all right. You should be so angry that your last conversation was an argument, that your last conversation with him could have been a permanent goodbye. Still, you drink in the air he makes electric, your heartbeat keeping swimmer's pace. You see how he's aged, come into a peaceful confidence.

"You saved us all," he says, gratitude warming his skin. He puts down his teacup and braids his fingers together in his lap. "We were having a huge fight at her parents' apartment that day, so none of us were inside the tower." Katrina, he adds, has left with her parents, gone back to North Carolina. For good. "But I'm staying on." He pauses. "I had to make a plan about everything before I saw you again."

Baba nods.

Taking a cream cracker from the plate and snapping it in two, Ma asks, "You'll be in town?" She starts to take a bite but stops.

"In between assignments," Crash replies, then brings the cup of tea to his lips.

"This is a big city." Her eyes are hot.

"In a free country," Crash says, his cup landing with a thud on the coffee table, some tea sloshing out and down the side.

"Don't start," you say as quietly as you can.

Baba rises from his seat, takes a napkin, and wipes the side of Crash's cup. "Our daughter no longer belongs to this family." His tone is as soft as the used napkin he places under Crash's mug, as a coaster.

You try not to react, you try not to think of Neel—even though he has broken your marriage contract, you are still not free.

"And yet she is here when I finally find her," Crash says.

Ma sighs audibly.

"That is a coincidence," you say, not looking at your parents or at Crash but at the cracker you've just crushed in your hand.

"You don't believe that," Crash says. He leans over, takes a fresh napkin from the table, and offers it to you.

When you reach for it, your fingers touch. A tiny bolt of electricity shoots through your veins. Your eyes lock. "No, I really don't."

The clock ticks loudly from the kitchen. "Things happen for a reason," he says.

"You sent the photograph," Ma says.

Crash nods. He rises and walks toward the front door and you cannot help but gape, you cannot hide your dismay. Baba mimics your face and sits frozen across from you. But Ma's face is an open wound, red and raw and full of pain. "Are you leaving?" Her voice is an old razor, rusty.

Crash picks up his backpack and returns to his chair. "No," he says. "I want to show you something." He pulls out a soft album.

Baba visibly relaxes and Ma crosses her arms.

You admire the sleek black case. His work portfolio.

"I wanted to show you what I've been doing," he says tenderly, laying open the flap, and turning it around so Ma and Baba can view his work right side up. "I have your daughter to thank."

You marvel at Crash, even now, his life's obsessions culled into one space, and how he gazes at the bewildering world through a single eye, the lens of his camera. His photographs astonish, a cardinal perched on the marble birdbath that's caught in the unexpected snow, the shadows cast in the hallway of his parents' home as the sun descends, the looks on the ROTC officers' faces as they lower the American flag at the end of the weekday. You marvel that Crash is talking as quickly as an auctioneer, without ever saying a single word.

"Things happen for a reason," you say again. A delivery truck backs up in the alley, a beeping that repeats for several seconds. "I've tried to remember that," you say, and picture his face the night his sister died, and look at him now—calm, mature.

Baba coughs again, this time into his fist.

"But you promised to be a good girl, Heera," Ma says, her voice as sharp as a butcher's knife, the steel cutting through the air.

You detect crow's-feet beginning to line the corners of Crash's eyes.

"She is being good," Baba says, his Bengali a murmuring brook heading toward a vast river. "She married the boy of our choice."

Crash looks to you for translation but you shake your head ever so slightly.

"Well, she can't mope about it now," Ma says in English, standing up and smoothing out her housecoat. "It's done, and . . . and Dia . . . Dia has a new life to build now."

You inhale sharply, you glance at Crash but his face is blank.

You and Ma look at each other, and you blink back the past. Marie is gone forever but in this moment, you have your parents once again.

The men reluctantly stand and crumbs fall from their laps onto the ground.

Baba says, "Thank you for coming, Crash." His gait is crooked as he steps toward the door.

Ma says, "Please come again." Her voice mechanical, an automated message. Her hands fly to her face, rub tears at the corners of her eyes. But you don't care, you are happy Ma is using long-ago language.

Crash looks around the room. "Where are the baby pictures?" he asks you, Ma, Baba. "She's got to be five months old now. Is she asleep?"

You gasp.

You shake your head.

Ma's face turns cherry red. Baba groans.

"I lost her," you say.

His squeezes shut his eyes. "I . . . I didn't know." He turns to them. "My condolences to you."

Baba answers, "Thank you."

You slip on your shoes. "I'll walk him to the subway."

"What if someone sees you?" Ma asks, as motionless as a mannequin.

"Here we are strangers," you say.

"Yes," Baba says. "In this city we do not know each other."

You point in the general direction of your room, your luggage and keys. "I'll come back for those."

"Please hurry," Ma says.

But Baba says, "Take your time."

"I won't keep her too long," Crash says.

᯽

You and Crash hold hands once you reach the bottom of the staircase, and push through the glass doors in the lobby. The street is not yet busy, a yellow delivery truck on the far corner, a taxi looking for a fare, the sun still climbing past the fire escapes and the old buildings, and the faded white sign that reads THE WAGES OF SIN IS DEATH. ROMANS 6:23.

Crash's heart thuds in your palm as your hand grips his. You want this moment to last forever.

You tug Crash to the right, away from the subway station.

"Why this way?" he asks. "My studio is in the other direction." His face is a palette of emotions: expectant, triumphant, and yet haunted. "I'm sorry back there, Dia."

You nod and squeeze his hand. You clear your throat. You think of your adventures over the years, how there was little proof aside from the *A*'s painted on water towers. "I have to make a stop," you say, remembering that Crash always carries around a camera, stashed in his backpack. "I have to document this first moment . . ."

He hears your tone, and salutes in return. "Where to, ma'am?"

"The Cloisters," you say, and laugh. You want to photograph him in the gardens, by the stone arches, by the stained glass; you want strangers to photograph the two of you. A couple.

He frowns. "That's far."

You shrug. "Maybe that's not far enough. Maybe we should go to Canada and start over."

"Your mother will kill me." He points a finger. "Right after she kills you."

You chuckle. "So you do care what happens to me?"

"Nah," he says, his face suddenly somber. "I just like watching their eyes pop."

You smile at him and he smiles in return. You stop at the curb and wait for the traffic light to change to green, and Crash looks the other direction. His gaze off you for a moment, you instantly wonder if you'll always be waiting. You think of Krishna's parents, waiting. You think of Ma and Baba, waiting. But then he looks at you and you forget everything, the dust of doubt vanishes.

"C'mon," he says, tugging you back toward the subway. "It's too early to go to the Bronx." He beams. "And Canada."

You follow him willingly, happily, blindly. You try to remember anything, something other than this moment of holding hands and walking together. The walk is at once unending and immediate.

You arrive at the station. Crash hesitates for a moment, then pushes you along, pays for your token and you pass single file through the turnstile. Your keys and bag are with your parents, Neel and your in-laws might as well be on the moon they are so far from your thoughts. And yet they suddenly weigh in. A chorus of voices poised to argue inside your mind. "I thought I was just walking you here," you say.

He takes your hand and raises it to his lips, and gives it a formal kiss. "I'll bring you back. One day."

You turn hot and cold at once, and begin trembling. "You have to go now, and we can make a plan for later." You stare up at his most familiar face.

"Not going anywhere without you," he says.

You shake your head. "You know I can't just leave like this. I told them I'd come back." You show him your ring, tell him the short version of Neel and Sarah and Kevin. "I have to talk to . . . all of my in-laws."

"I'll come with you," he says.

You shake your head. "I have to do this task alone."

His eyes flash. "All I know is that it's been five years, eleven months, two weeks, and a day since everything went to hell, and those times we ran into each other don't count."

You sigh. "In fifty years, it'll be a small fraction." You squeeze his hand. "I just have to go back and talk to them."

He gathers you in his arms and dips you backwards as if at the end of a dance. "Save the math, Dia," he says, his voice loud. Commuters coming through the turnstile turn their heads slightly to watch. "In the next hour, everything might change. You know that as well as I do." His arms are strong. Crash smiles for a second, his nod to the audience of strangers is almost imperceptible except that you see it, clear and sure as if you are watching the opening credits of a film at the theater.

You shudder. You can no longer live at the margins, wondering, guessing, hoping. You think of Neel, and his choices. You cannot miss another moment of your own life. "Come back with me, Crash."

He shakes his head. "What good will come from that?"

You exhale. "They'll see our happy faces, they'll see that we're not kidding," you whisper.

He grips tighter. "I'm not letting you out of my sight."

You laugh. "Except when you're on assignment halfway across the world."

He lifts you back to a standing position, pulls you along toward the exit and back to your parents. "I mean when we eventually talk to my mom."

Your ears listen to an echo. "Your mother doesn't scare me." You pause. "Well, not too much."

Entrance

THIS IS THE WAY IT SHOULD HAVE BEEN SIX YEARS AGO, YOU in college, the future a road trip with a sunny day and a full tank of gas and endless possibilities. Ma and Baba, having dropped you off at your dormitory at the beginning of the semester, coming to visit on Parents' Weekend, Marie as your roommate, Crash as your first boyfriend. You waving goodbye to the past and promising to call.

You are now on your way to community college classes, free of your in-laws and your dead but not dead husband. You pledge to your mother not to pickpocket anymore, to find a job. You pledge to yourself to divorce expeditiously, but not remarry too quickly—or at all. For now, you live in a rented room near the college. But this day, on your birthday, you wake up in your parents' apartment. You a birthday girl and this city alive in celebration of All Hallows' Eve, money in your pocket that Baba gave you this morning for your twenty-fourth. You tell Ma that you have two stops to make tonight: to light a candle for Marie and to see Crash, that you will have your birthday dinner with them tomorrow.

You are not at peace, for Ma's eyes narrow and she swallows hard.

You feel the old rebellion rise up inside you.

Still it is a truce, for she says after a long pause, "Don't stay out too late. This isn't Raleigh, Dia."

You walk into Tiny's Costume Warehouse. You shed your skin, albeit temporarily, at the back of store, where racks and racks of "girl" costumes are haphazardly strewn.

The poor lighting but high ceilings give the feel of a modern stage. A place where at any moment an amateur acting troupe of philosophy students might take over like an invading army, trying on other people's clothes and thoughts to see if the words and costumes fit, cheek by jowl, on their own skins. Someone, or perhaps many, before you tried on costume after costume — but didn't bother to rehang them. Tiny turns out to be a short but obese man with a full head of mouse-colored hair and angry brown eyes. He says the last girl in here settled on an expensive Judy Jetson dress — after making this ever-expanding mess.

You admire a leopard-skin "Jungle Jane" dress from the Tarzan era, with spaghetti straps and tight skirt. Too short. On a mannequin, a hoop skirt, something Scarlett O'Hara might have worn in *Gone with the Wind*. You finger the pale lace attached to the hem.

Something glitters close to the bottom of a nearby pile.

Curious, you uncover a breastplate, and along with it a short, white, toga-style dress. You turn to Tiny, ever present and ever watchful. "This is a girl's outfit? What, a female gladiator?" The high girded skirt trembles in your hands.

He shakes his head, his smile taut and bored. "Amazon. There are fake bows and arrows in that pile, too. Somewhere."

"Amazon!" You search for the rest, then hand over the cash. You clutch a fake sword in your hand as he rings up the breastplate and the skirt. You ask for the key to the restroom to change.

"Don't get on the train with that blade," Tiny says. "You'll get arrested."

You smile, and nod.

You walk many blocks toward your college. Everyone is out already: dressed as magicians, mimes, cartoon characters, punk rock stars, mermaids, nuns. Men in wedding gowns wearing veils and holding trains, women as Frankenstein's monster's bride or female Dracula, a pair of men as characters from a long-running wine cooler commercial, and a woman in a billowing gown that reminds you of Catherine in *Wuthering Heights*. You pass a group of people clustered together, frowning and wearing purple from head to foot. Sour grapes. You spy a man in a toga with an open bottle of wine. From the side it could be Crash, same build, same height, same wavy hair.

You almost greet him by name, but something inside you stops.

He turns around, and you lock eyes with a stranger. "I'm Dionysus," he says, then drinks from the bottle.

You say something nice, though you think he looks suspiciously like a parody of John Belushi's character in *Animal House*. You glance at your watch and know it's too early, Crash will not arrive for another two hours. You think you spy Marie as you exit Broadway to cut across to your college: a tall girl with her shade of honey blond, her long-legged stride. She is dressed all in black, her cape waving behind her like a flag, walking toward a cluster of buildings backlit by the sun. At first you try to catch up, to get a better look, to call out to her, to tell her that you turned out okay, to tell her that you're finally free.

But your costume becomes heavier and heavier. You slow your pace, you try to control your breathing.

You know it's not her, you know that you carry Marie in your heart, that she lives on each time you remember her. You take a deep breath and stop on the sidewalk, step into the grass and allow the people behind you to pass. You stand still until there are so many costumed bodies around you, until you are in the middle of a strange and wonderful sea. You stand still until that girl is out of your line of vision, until she disappears.

Acknowledgments

Thank you all for reading and for keeping Susan's memory alive. Gratitude to my wonderful agent, Reiko Davis, and all the efforts of DeFiore & Co.'s Meredith Kaffel Simonoff, Miriam Altshuler and Adam Schear, Linda Kaplan, Emma Haviland-Blunk. Many thanks to my editors Pilar Garcia-Brown and Rakia Clark for their love. Thanks to the Houghton Mifflin Harcourt and HarperCollins family for all the support, including Emma Gordon, Andrea DeWerd, Liz Anderson, Martha Kennedy, Laura Brady, Rachael DeShano, Ana Deboo, Emily Snyder, Chloe Foster, Ivy Givens, and Rita Cullen.

Enormous gratitude to my sister-writers Elizabeth Stark and Sejal Patel for their heroic efforts—I wouldn't have finished this novel during a pandemic without your generosity. My thanks to friends and storytellers without whose company I would be bereft: Elizabeth Rosner, Nayomi Munaweera, Dorothy Hearst, Jon Krim, David Woolbright, Angie Powers, Tesha and Parna Sengupta and their parents; Sarah Kobrinsky, Lucy Jane Bledsoe, Ellen Sussman, Julie Rappaport, Deb Krainin; my classmates at Book Writing World, UTV, FMWG+B & CWOV Crazy 8s; and to my wonderful VONA friends, especially Karineh Mahdessian, Cinelle Barnes, Sarah Gonzalez, Vanessa Martir, Claire Calderon. Thanks to Amanda Gersh and Michael Howells, Louise Windsor, Dean and Kathy Brewer, Robin Holtson, Chris Evans,

Amanda Scacchitti, Linda Hosek, Dave Nast, Rajiv Mohabir, Anjoli Roy and family, Lea McLees, Jill Leonard, Luchina Fisher, Vicki Ferris, David McKinnis, Enrique and Clara Balorya, Matteo Ancona, Lane Mitchell, Beth Lyon, Felicia Ward, Maureen Fan, Monique Truong, Sunanda McGarvey and Subir Roy, Sharmistha and Arup Bose, Shankar and Ruma Sengupta, Laura and Erich Wefing, Kathy McDonald, Dani Chiofalo, Beth Woodward, Eric and Helen Graben, Joyce Fitzpatrick, Jeff and Cheryl Gramling, Elmaz Abinader and Molly Fisk.

Many thanks to Janet Fitch, Megha Majumdar, Anjali Enjeti, Zeyn Joukhadar, Maya Shanbhag Lang, and Kirthana Ramisetti for their enthusiasm and kindness. Thank you to all my teachers over the years, and especially to the poet Lucille Clifton for her friendship.

Love and gratitude to my husband, Joy, and our daughters, Anjini, Ellora, and Devrani; and to the Bagchi, Roychowdhury, Gupta, Nandi, Chakrabarti, Dasgupta, Laskar, and Sen families; most especially to A. L. and Renu Laskar, Pranab and Gauri Sen; Ru and Kimmy Sen, Raja and Shilpi Laskar, Aloke Chakravarty and the Saturday family reunions; Korinne Lassiter, Stephen Mcphaul, Faith Hoople, Ashmita Chatterjee and her wonderful family, Trisha Chakrabarti, Ryan Smith, Pete and Patricia Apostolakis; Jay and Tanya Kruse, Jurgen and Gloria Hofler. Thank you, Jay Chaudhuri and family, and the Ghosh and Bhattacharyya families of long-ago Raleigh. Remembering my grandparents, Mrs. Kalyani Sen and J. R. and Nilima Dasgupta, every day.